The Volcano's Going to Blow ...!

"Keith, what's happening?" Colleen demanded.
"The engines aren't responding!"

At the edge of his field-of-view, Keith could see giant Jupiter hanging in the sky, its cyclonic Great Red Spot staring down at him like a bloody eye. The level on the seismometer continued to climb. He desperately tried to activate the thrusters again, but without effect.

Suddenly, the seismometer data spiked to a value that triggered a yellow alarm. At the same instant the thrusters came to life, lifting the spacecraft from the rumbling face of Emakong.

"Come on..."

The surface of Io was receding, but the numbers on the altimeter were climbing too slowly. Suddenly, all the alarms flashed red.

Everything went dark.

TALES FROM THE WONDER ZONE

Stardust
•
Explorer
•
Orbiter

More Science Fiction
from Trifolium Books Inc.

**Packing Fraction
& Other Tales of Science
and Imagination**

Orbiter

Edited by
Julie E. Czerneda

Illustrated by
Jean-Pierre Normand

Trifolium Books Inc.
Toronto, Canada

We acknowledge the financial support of the Government of Canada
through the Book Publishing Industry Development Program (BPIDP) for
our publishing activities.

Canadian Cataloguing in Publication Data
Main entry under title:
     Orbiter
(Tales from the wonder zone)
ISBN 1-55244-020-6
1. Children's stories, American. 2. Children's stories, Canadian (English)
3. Science fiction, American. 4. Science fiction, Canadian (English)
I. Czerneda, Julie, 1955– II. Normand, Jean-Pierre III. Series.

PZ5.O72 2002   j813'.08762089282   C00-931743-0

Trifolium Books Inc.
195 Allstate Parkway,
Markham, Ontario L3R 4T8
godwit@fitzhenry.ca   www.fitzhenry.ca

Cover Design and Illustrations: Jean-Pierre Normand
Text Design: John Lee, Heidy Lawrance Associates

Printed in Canada
9 8 7 6 5 4 3 2 1

Dedications

Julie E. Czerneda: To Jim Rogerson and all those who worked tirelessly to see this project take flight, including Trudy Rising, Dawn Morin, Heidy Lawrance, and Beth Crane. To the talented and enthusiastic contributors. To David Brin, for his wonderful support and the introduction to this book. And to Jean-Pierre, for his awesome vision of our future.

Jean-Pierre Normand: To my parents, Marcel Normand and Bernadette Morin, who made it all possible for me.

Eric Choi: Special thanks to the Commune and Carbide-Tipped Pens writing groups, Rocky Persaud, and Bonnie and Kenny Choi for reviewing my story and providing invaluable suggestions.

Annette Griessman: For Alex and Kayla with love. And a special thanks to Julie for her faith in me.

Mark Canter: To my sons, Orion Sky Canter and Blake River Canter, artists and scientists of the 21st Century.

Jean-Louis Trudel: To my father, who introduced me to the life of the mind, with special thanks to the Commune and to the Centre interuniversitaire de recherche en science et en technologie for its technical support.

Anne Bishop: For Julie Czerneda, whose timely invitation helped this story come into being, and for Maggie Rogers and Cass Brunner.

CONTENTS

A Special Introduction by David Brin   ix

Just Like Being There by Eric Choi   1

Space Divers by Annette Griessman   21

Dragonfly by Mark Canter   39

Tether by Jean-Louis Trudel   59

A Strand in the Web by Anne Bishop   77

A Special Introduction by David Brin

There are some lies we're often told by cynics and sourpuss types. One of the worst is when they say you can't have everything.

If you want adventure, you can't think. If you think, you can't have fun. If it's educational, it must be boring. Friendship and romance never mix.

And a story that opens our eyes can't be any good as a story.

Of course, many of us have always — in our secret hearts — known otherwise. Those who think it's possible to do better. Those who look around and see some human progress, despite countless troubles we inherit from our parents' generation. Those who think that problems sometimes have solutions, and solutions can be found by those who search.

Whether or not this outlook is *right*, it has one definite advantage. It's more *fun* to believe in than the stylish cynicism of those who lean against walls, wearing a curl-lipped sneer, scoffing at those who try to make a better world.

Moreover, we had *better* believe it, if we want to find those solutions!

All right, that may be a crackpot idea. But science fiction was born amid the crazy notion of problem-solving progress. Even the dire warning cries of Mary Shelley's *Frankenstein* and George Orwell's *1984* come with this moral — implicit between the lines — that people don't have to make the same mistakes that characters in the novel make. We don't have to take the same dark roads. In fact, reading and imagining dark futures may be one of the best ways to help future generations avoid them.

Albert Einstein had a word for this ... *Gedanken experiment* ... or "thought experiment." Trying to imagine what might happen if we do *this* instead of *that*. We all do it every day, when we fantasize about how others might react to the things we're about to say or do. Trying to project the possible consequences of our actions, so we can avoid making some mistakes. It doesn't always work. Sometimes mistakes happen anyway — live and learn. Still, it's worth trying to do, all the time.

That is what science fiction is about, at its deepest heart — exploring possible or plausible tomorrows, attempting to understand what *change* might do to us, to our societies, to those we love. At its best, it has all of the best features of literature — fascinating characters, events, action, emotions — but also with this added feature found nowhere else: a relentless interest in the consequences of change.

That's where "science" comes into the picture, because the vast increase in human knowledge seems to be driving change ever faster. Even if 90% of these developments are good, that leaves a lot of potential harm we must explore with our minds, working out the problems *before* they come true to bite us!

Hence, the great value of anthologies like *Orbiter.* The stories contained in this volume — many of them written by members of the coming generation — emphasize twin themes of spaceflight and biology, two subjects that may seem at odds. But the more we learn about what it takes to maintain life in this harsh cosmos, the more it seems apparent that the physical sciences and life sciences must live together, operating hand-in-hand.

The first story, "Just Like Being There," by Eric Choi, takes a look at the notion of exploring space through *telepresence.* We have learned that sending live human beings to far planets may be horribly dangerous and expensive. Solving the problems — enabling our children to colonize the solar system — may take a bit of time. Meanwhile though, we'll continue sending ahead scouts: not only robots, but machines that help real explorers touch and feel faraway locales, bringing human thought and judgment to strange worlds many years before we actually get to set foot there.

Plans for telerobotic survey craft are already leaving the drawing boards. Through groups such as the Planetary Society, it will enable many of you, holding this book, to take a turn at controlling a little robot, perhaps on Mars or the Moon.

Annette Griessman's "Space Divers," goes back to the kind of stories I grew up with, that were written in the "golden age" of science fiction — a terrific tale about space explorers in peril, figuring out how to use the very laws of nature to save their own lives. Along similar lines, "Tether" by Jean-Louis Trudel takes a step further into the physics that has started to affect space designs more recently.

Finally, two stories push the emphasis further afield from space technology over to issues of life itself — how explorers may face basic issues of biology or ecology when they set sail across the cosmos. Mark Canter's "Dragonfly" takes the reader on a stunning ride, forcing a change in perspective to the point of view of a plucky little astronaut, smaller than a bug, but more formidable than a rhino! While Anne Bishop's "A Strand in the Web" is the longest tale in the book, its serious themes of responsibility and destiny are softened by a strong sense of personal character, as the crew of a doomed starship struggle to bring life back to a wounded world.

Why did the authors spend their time, energy, and creativity to write these stories? If you've ever sweated over a made-up tale, you'll know that no amount of money can explain why people strive to invent new worlds and vivid people to inhabit them, striving against adversities with both courage and cunning. Part of it expresses an urge to teach ... to pass on a sense of wonder that they picked up from earlier authors!

But above all, there is the sheer joy of it. The pleasure of exploring ideas and pouring a part of yourself — however briefly — into a future when problems might be solved by both thoughtfulness and bold action. This is as intensely human as anything else about our amazing species. As long as there is change, there will be brave spirits ready to face it, arming themselves with knowledge and forging ahead to adventure.

David Brin

Dr. David Brin is the award-winning author of the Uplift Storm Trilogy, *Foundation's Triumph*, and *Kiln People*.

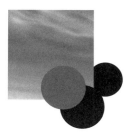

Just Like Being There

by Eric Choi

Io was a bad place for something to go wrong.

The fifth of Jupiter's twenty-eight moons, Io was deep inside a zone of radiation produced by solar particles trapped in the gas giant's magnetic field. Heated by the gravitational tug-of-war between Jupiter and its outer moons, the volcanoes that covered its surface erupted almost constantly, sending plumes of sulfur hundreds of kilometers into space.

1

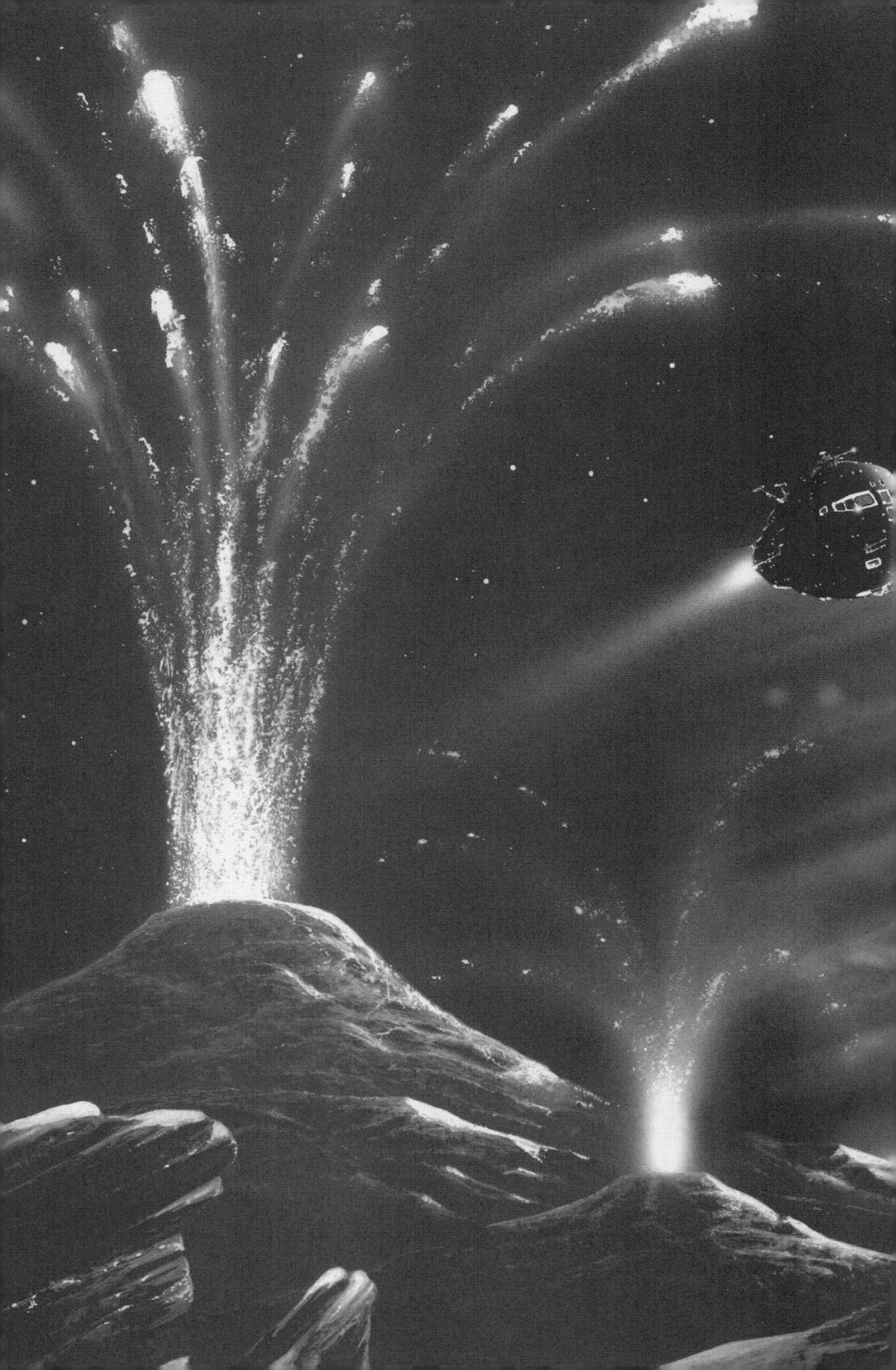

Keith Mackay's spacecraft had landed on Io, and it was in trouble.

The spacecraft had touched down in a volcano called Emakong Patera with a not-so-soft landing that threw up a large cloud of sulfur. But according to the mission schedule, it should have landed ten minutes ago, well before Keith linked-in with the ansible machine. He immediately checked the seismometer, and one look at its peaks told him this was a bad time to visit.

"I have to get out of here."

"What's the problem?" crackled the voice of Flight Director Colleen Hodge through his headset.

"The volcano's gonna blow." Keith pulled the stick and the thrusters responded, lifting the spacecraft off the surface.

A split second later, the engines died. The spacecraft came crashing down, kicking up another cloud of sulfur.

"What's going on?" He pulled the stick again. Nothing happened.

"Keith, what's happening?" Colleen demanded.

"The engines aren't responding!"

At the edge of his field-of-view, Keith could see giant Jupiter hanging in the sky, its cyclonic Great Red Spot staring down at him like a bloody eye. The level on the seismometer continued to climb. He desperately tried to activate the thrusters again, but without effect.

Suddenly, the seismometer data spiked to a value that triggered a yellow alarm. At the same instant the thrusters came to life, lifting the spacecraft away from the rumbling face of Emakong.

"Come on…"

The surface of Io was receding, but the numbers on the altimeter were climbing too slowly. Suddenly, all the alarms flashed red.

Everything went dark.

Keith ripped off his virtual-reality equipment and slumped in his seat. The alarms that flashed on the ansible machine only told him the obvious — the instantaneous communication link with TeleProbe-42 was broken. He stared at his console, but the blank screen offered no further answers.

"Keith, please report to my office," said Colleen over his headset.

He packed up his veergear, shut down the console, and quietly made his way out of Mission Control. Most of the virtual-reality astronauts, or "veernauts," were busy operating other TeleProbes across the Solar System. The few who weren't turned to watch Keith leave, nodding silent sympathy.

The walls of Colleen Hodge's office were covered with pictures of astronauts and a colourful assortment of mission logos. It was like a museum of the bygone era of human space exploration. Out of the corner of his eye Keith spotted the crew portrait for the Ares 7 mission — the one with his dad in it. He looked away.

"What happened?" Colleen asked.

"I don't know, but everything was all wrong from the start. According to the schedule, TP-42 should have landed ten minutes earlier, but when I established the ansible link it had just touched down. And when I tried to take off—"

Colleen interrupted. "Why were you trying to take off so soon?"

"I told you, Emakong Patera was going to blow. I could tell from the seismometer data."

Colleen looked skeptical.

"I'm a geologist. I *know*." Keith continued, "So, that's when I tried to take off … but the thrusters wouldn't respond. I kept trying. Nothing happened until the yellow alarm went off, but by then, it was too late."

"Landing on a volcano, on the most volcanically active body in the Solar System …" Colleen shook her head. "I knew it was a crazy idea from the start."

"Emakong had been dormant for ten months. It's just bad luck it went active now."

"We can't fly missions based on luck."

"But I thought that was the point of using robots!" Keith protested. "We can take greater risks, go places we couldn't —"

"All right, all right." Colleen glanced at the clock. "We should be getting the radio data in about forty-five minutes. Then we'll have a better idea of what happened. In the meantime, I'm going to call in the failure investigation team. Unfortunately, this means you're off flight status pending the outcome of the inquiry. Don't take it personally, okay? Nobody's saying it's your fault, but —"

"It's standard procedure.... I understand."

"In the meantime," Colleen continued, "I'm temporarily reassigning you to the Public Affairs Office."

"Great," Keith muttered sarcastically. "Just great."

Keith's first assignment in his unwanted transfer to Public Affairs was to do a talk for students at Jefferson Davis High School. While preparing for the presentation in his office, his vidphone rang. He glanced at the number and groaned.

"Hi, Dad."

Rob Mackay was 53 years old, and had settled down to retire in Canberra, Australia. Despite the years, he still resembled the stereotypical astronaut. His once-brown crew-cut hair was now white, but he still had that steely-eyed, square-jawed look. Ten years ago, he had been the flight engineer on Ares 7 — the last human Mars landing. During a solar storm, he had courage-ously stayed outside the ship's shelter to repair the engines in time for a crucial course correction maneuver.

"Hi, Keith." There was a split-second time delay as the signal was relayed by communications satellite across the Pacific. "I heard about TP-42, and I wanted to see how you were doing."

Keith gritted his teeth. NASA released news on the Web *way* too fast for his liking.

"I lost ansible contact while trying to abort the Io landing. We'll have a better idea what happened when we get some radio data back."

"Well, these things happen," Rob said. "I remember when I was on Mars, and I accidentally —"

"You accidentally pointed the camera at the Sun and fried it. Dad, I've heard this story a thousand times." Keith frowned. "Are you saying I screwed up?"

"No! I was just —"

"Look Dad, I'm really busy. They stuck me in Public Affairs, and I've got to prepare this talk for some high school kids."

"I understand. I'm … I'm sorry to have bothered you." He smiled weakly. "Take care, son."

Keith hung up the vidphone.

Twenty students attended Keith's talk at Davis High. Sixteen were physically present, while the remaining four were linked-in from remote sites. Bright, young, and ambitious, each of them came to hear about the dream of space exploration.

It was a dream that had almost died.

Following close calls on the Ares 4 and 7 Mars missions, and then the Clavius Moonbase disaster, the US Congress had passed legislation prohibiting NASA from sending astronauts beyond Earth orbit. Out of the ashes of the human deep–space exploration program, the TeleProbe project had been born.

Keith began his talk. "The biggest problem in operating spacecraft by remote control is the time delay. A radio signal takes 2.7 seconds to go from the Earth to the Moon and back. For Mars, the round-trip delay can be up to 40 minutes, and for Jupiter and the outer planets, you're talking hours.

"To get around this, TeleProbes use two special technologies: the remote agent, and a machine called an ansible." Keith showed a flowchart. "The remote agent is a sophisticated computer program that allows a TeleProbe to fly itself for long periods without contact from Mission Control. We only need to give the TeleProbe general instructions, like 'land on that asteroid', and the remote agent plans, schedules, and then executes everything needed to make it happen. It can even recognize and avoid hazards."

Keith displayed a diagram. "The second special technology is the ansible. This machine gives us limited periods of instantaneous communication with the Tele-Probe. By removing the time delay, we can do things like field geology or other complex, hands-on tasks by remote control — things that used to require the physical presence of an astronaut."

"How much time does an ansible give you?" asked a student named Vikhram Ganesh.

"The ansible works on a theory called quantum entanglement," Keith explained. "The TeleProbes carry a supply of entangled photons, or light particles, that are 'linked' in a quantum mechanical way to a corresponding supply in the ansibles at Mission Control.

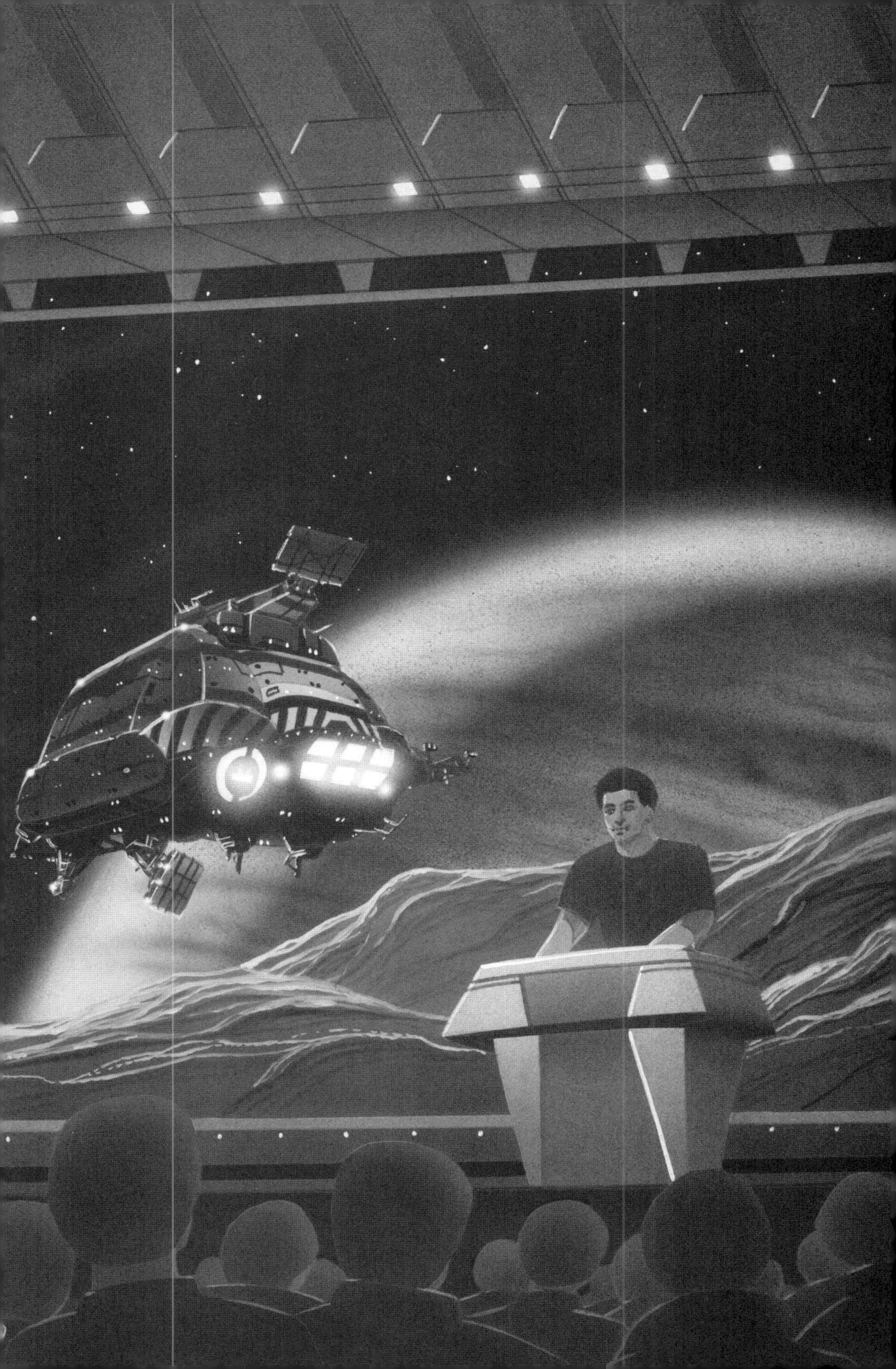

Instantaneous communication is possible until the states of all the photons have been determined — until they've all been used up. Depending on the data resolution, that's usually between two to three hours."

One of the remote-linked students, Susan Fontaine, asked a question. "What scientific instruments do the TeleProbes carry?"

"The TeleProbes use a simple design based on commercially available parts to reduce cost. Generally, TeleProbes carry scientific instruments like stereoscopic cameras, spectrometers, seismometers, radar ... a standard set of science instruments."

Susan continued, "I saw this program on DiscoverNet the other night. They were interviewing a veernaut named Wendy —"

"Wendy Chong." Keith narrowed his eyes. Wendy had quit the veernaut corps last year. "What was the interview about?"

"She said the TeleProbes were too limited to do useful geological work. She talked about the time she was operating TeleProbe-34 on Mars and she discovered this unusual rock, but because of the sensor limitations she couldn't figure out if it was an igneous, an impact breccia, or a sedimentary type of rock."

"Wow!" Keith was impressed. "I'm amazed you know so much about geology."

"Thanks. Anyway, the problem was that each identification of the type of rock would have supported a different theory about the geologic history of the site. She said that an astronaut could have identified the rock in a few minutes, like on Ares 7 when Marv Shapley and — hey, wasn't your dad on that mission?"

The eyes of all the students suddenly lit up.

"Yeah, my dad was on Ares 7," Keith said at last. He changed the subject. "Remember though, each TeleProbe costs ten times less than a human mission, so even if there are some limitations I'd say it's a good deal." He took a deep breath. "Believe me, when you're in ansible mode at the highest data resolution, with the full virtual-reality gear, it's just like being there."

Upon his return to NASA, Keith went to Colleen's office to get the latest on the investigation. The news was not good.

"We've lost radio contact with TeleProbe-42," she said. "Taking into account the time delay, the signal ended at the same time you lost the ansible link. Also, the Shapley Observatory has confirmed that Emakong Patera did erupt."

Keith's face fell. "But we have data up until then?"

"Yes." Plots were slowly appearing on Colleen's computer. "The engineers have started analyzing it. So far, they haven't found any obvious mechanical malfunctions."

"Looks like some of the electronics were already starting to fail because of the radiation," Keith observed. "But the remote agent did switch to the backups like it's supposed to."

"There's a chance TP-42 survived," Colleen said. "We're going to use the Deep Space Network antennas to try to reestablish radio contact over the weekend. But with forty-seven operational TeleProbes across the Solar System taking priority, we'll only be able to make periodic attempts."

"Is there anything I can do?"

Colleen shrugged. "Cross your fingers and hope for better news on Monday."

Keith couldn't wait that long. Throughout the weekend, he contacted NASA every couple of hours, trying to get the latest news. Finally, he got a call from Colleen ordering him to leave the engineers alone.

On Monday, as Keith was driving into the NASA parking lot, his phone rang. Recognizing his parents' number, he muted the handset. He'd get back to them when he had time.

Moments later in Colleen's office, he learned that crossing his fingers hadn't helped.

"The Deep Space Network wasn't able to reestablish radio contact," she told him. "NASA Headquarters has officially declared the TeleProbe-42 mission over. If it wasn't destroyed in the eruption, the radiation must have fried all its electronics by now."

Keith couldn't hide his disappointment. "But we still don't know why I couldn't take off."

"No, but the engineers did find something odd." Colored lines traced horizontally across Colleen's computer screen, like the vital signs of a patient. She pointed. "See that? An unscheduled thruster firing."

"That's too big for a course correction maneuver." Keith thought for a moment. "TeleProbe remote agents are designed to automatically avoid hazards. TP-42's agent knew it had to avoid flying through volcanic plumes. That looks like a plume avoidance maneuver."

"But according to the pictures from the Shapley Observatory, there weren't any erupting volcanoes along the probe's descent course."

"So why did TP-42 fire its engines?"

"We don't know."

When Keith returned to his office, he found a message on his system from his mother. It was text only, just a few lines long, but he took several minutes to digest its contents. When he finally dialed the vidphone, his hands were almost trembling.

"Wooden Hospital."

"Could you put me through to Victor Poulos' room?" The pseudonym was no doubt intended to keep the reporters away, at least for a little while.

A moment later his father appeared on the screen.

"Keith!"

"I ... I got the message from Mom," he stammered. "Dad ... you've got cancer?"

Rob Mackay nodded.

Keith felt confused and afraid. "What ... What kind of cancer?"

"Thyroid," his father replied. "I guess I couldn't dodge the bullet forever. According to the doctor — Dr. Albacea's

13

her name — it's probably related to the radiation I was exposed to during that solar storm on the Ares 7 mission."

"What's going to happen?"

"Dr. Albacea says they're going to map my DNA so they can genetically tailor the treatment to me."

Keith shook his head. "It … it's just not fair. I'm getting so upset about losing a TeleProbe, me sitting here every day on a comfy chair in an air-conditioned Mission Control, while you … you had to risk —"

"Keith, listen to me. What I did — what all of us astronauts did — was important. If you ask me, we're still needed out there. I have no regrets about any of it. Just to have the chance to stand on Mars, to look up in an alien sky and see two moons … I wouldn't change a thing."

He looked away for a moment. "I have to go. Dr. Albacea's here. Looks like it's time for more tests."

Keith nodded.

"Thanks so much for calling."

"Dad…" Keith touched the screen, but all he felt was cold glass.

"Keith, whatever happens … I want you to know that I'm very proud of you." He smiled weakly. "Talk to you soon."

Keith just sat there, staring at the blank vidphone screen. *What is it with me and Dad? Am I mad at him for being away so much when I was small? But Dad was always there for me when it counted.*

Or … could I actually be jealous of him, because he's actually been out there while I just shadow box in virtual-reality? Keith was overcome with shame. *Am I really so petty? Just because I'll never have a chance to see two moons in an alien sky....*

Keith blinked. Mars had two moons, Phobos and Deimos. At last count Jupiter had twenty-eight. The four largest innermost moons, including Io, were called the Galilean satellites after their discoverer, the Italian astronomer Galileo. The four largest moons....

He set up a simulation on his computer and ran it. The Galilean moons waltzed about Jupiter in their Newtonian dance. He zoomed in on TeleProbe-42's course and changed the field-of-view to what the spacecraft would have seen on approach.

There was the answer.

"Thanks, Dad." Keith wiped his eyes with the back of his hand, grateful to be alone.

"The failure investigation team has concluded that your theory is the most likely explanation for the loss of TeleProbe-42."

Colleen was telling Keith the engineers' findings, but he really wasn't listening.

"Europa, the next moon out, briefly appeared on Io's horizon in the field-of-view of TP-42's horizon scanner. This fooled the remote agent into performing a thruster burn to avoid what it thought was the plume from an erupting volcano. The course change was small, but it was enough to delay the landing by ten minutes and forty seconds.

15

"When you cut in with the ansible, the remote agent was still finishing up the landing sequence of its program. So when you tried to take off, it interpreted the thruster firing as a malfunction and shut them down. It finally commanded a takeoff itself when the sensor data met its danger criteria — a level that was higher than yours, which was based on human experience.

"But by then, it was too late. TP-42 was probably destroyed in the eruption of Emakong Patera.

"So, that's it. A simple computer error ended your mission." Colleen shrugged. "It's unfortunate remote agent commands override ansible commands. The TeleProbe designers felt that since the spacecraft would know best what its immediate environment was like..."

"Every machine needs an off button," Keith muttered, "and someone to push it." He looked at his father's picture. "Does this mean I'm back on flight status?"

"Of course." Colleen frowned. "You've been awfully quiet, Keith. Are you all right?"

"My dad's been diagnosed with thyroid cancer."

"*What?*" Colleen exclaimed. "Why wasn't I informed —"

"I'm sorry." Keith stood up quickly. "I've got to go."

The suborbital flight from Houston to Canberra took 45 minutes. Stuck in traffic, the taxi ride to Wooden Hospital took an hour. The irony of the drive taking longer than the trip across the Pacific was not lost to Keith as the cab pulled into the hospital.

He met Dr. Penny Albacea in the hall outside his father's
room.

"We've tailored the monoclonal antibodies to his
genetic profile," she explained. "These antibodies deliver
the chemotherapy directly to the cancer cells. So far,
your father is responding well to the treatment."

"But if this doesn't work, his thyroid will have to be
removed," Keith stated, "He'll have to go on hormone
replacement therapy for the rest of his life."

"That used to be the only option," Dr. Albacea
nodded. "But with any luck, your father's thyroid will
function normally again."

"Thank you, doctor."

Dr. Albacea gave Keith a pat on the shoulder before she
walked away. He watched her disappear down the corridor,
then opened the door to his father's room and entered.

"Keith!"

"Hi, Dad."

"Well, this is a pleasant surprise."

Keith was glad to see his father still had his hair. He
pulled up a chair.

"How do you feel?"

"Well, I don't think the cancer will kill me," Rob said.
"The food'll do it first."

Keith smiled at the corny remark.

"So," his father said, "you're back on flight status."

"That's right."

"What's your next mission?"

"TeleProbe-56. It will arrive at Venus in February. Maybe
I'll find out why the surface of Venus looks to be all about

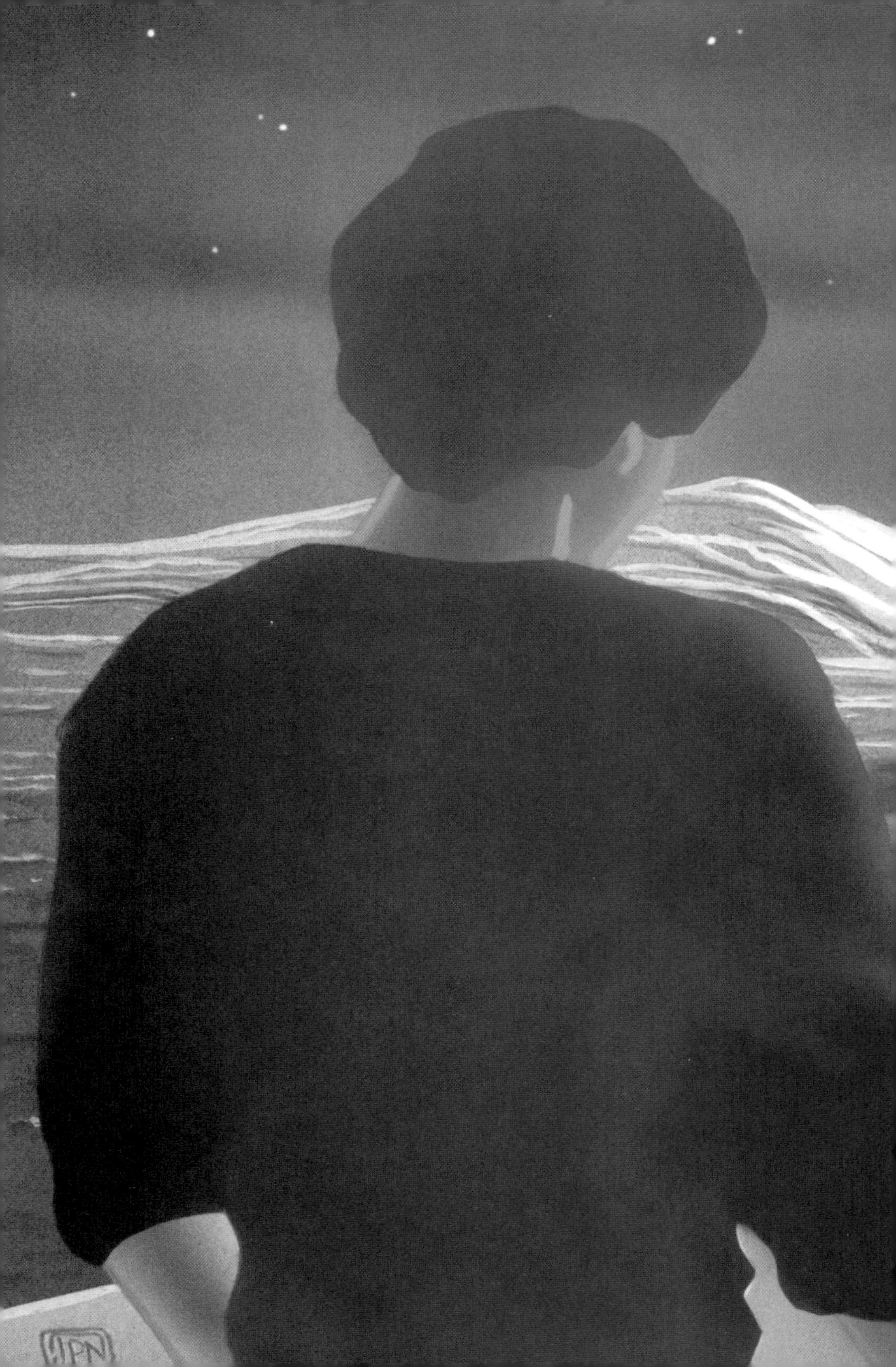

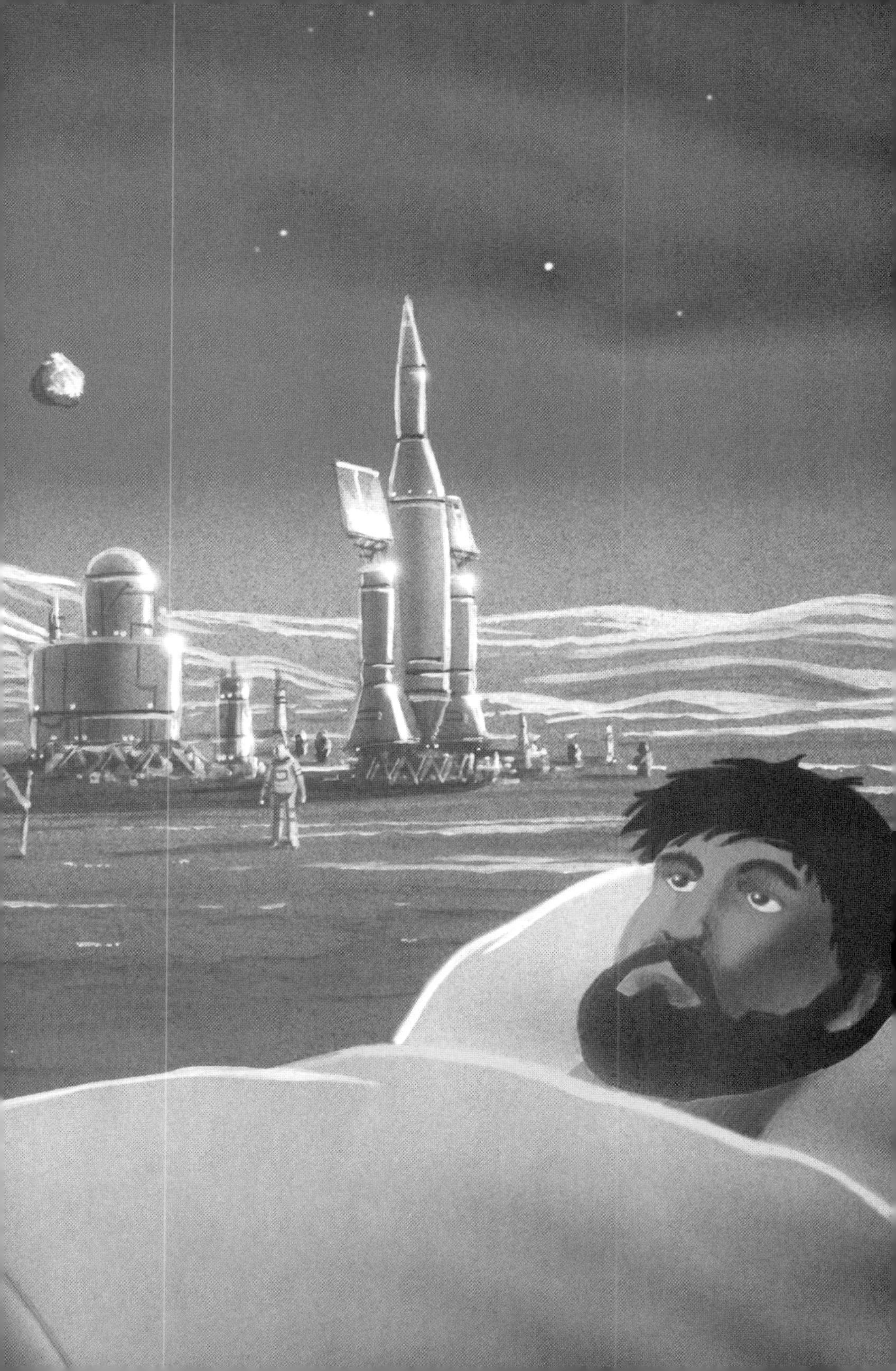

the same age. Some geologists think Venus sort of cata-strophically erupts every couple of thousand years, resur-facing the whole planet with magma. Maybe I'll get a chance to see if this is true. Unfortunately, I'll only have half an hour to do it before the probe dies."

"You'll be lucky to get half an hour. Sulfuric acid clouds, hot enough to melt lead on the surface... Nice place to visit —"

"But I wouldn't want to go there!"

Father and son shared a moment of laughter.

"Dad...What was it like ... to walk on Mars?"

He raised his eyebrows. "Oh, I'm sure you've heard me ramble about that a thousand times."

"No, I haven't," Keith said quietly.

He thought for a moment. "Well, I could move around very easily, since Mars' gravity is only about three-eights that of Earth. It felt really comfortable, even in my heavy spacesuit..."

Suddenly Rob Mackay stopped talking, and bowed his head. When he spoke again, it was in a very different tone of voice. "I'll tell you what it was like. It felt like I was dreaming. I kept wondering when I was going to wake up. It was like ... it was like when I was a little boy, and my Dad would tell me a wonderful bedtime story. Walking on Mars was the most wonderful story of my life."

Keith put his arms around his father, and held him tight.

It still took a person to be a hero.

Space Divers

by Annette Griessman

Tessa brushed dust from the rock before her carefully, trying to see the features hidden beneath. She sighed with contentment and sat back. This was heaven, she thought. A mystery in the depths of space. She paused for a moment to look up from her work.

The view of the satiny blue planet revolving beneath took her breath away. But it didn't create as much wonder as the blanket of asteroids that encircled the world like a lacy, protective shell. She was secured to one of the asteroids now — a large, dark one covered with deep, sharp-edged grooves.

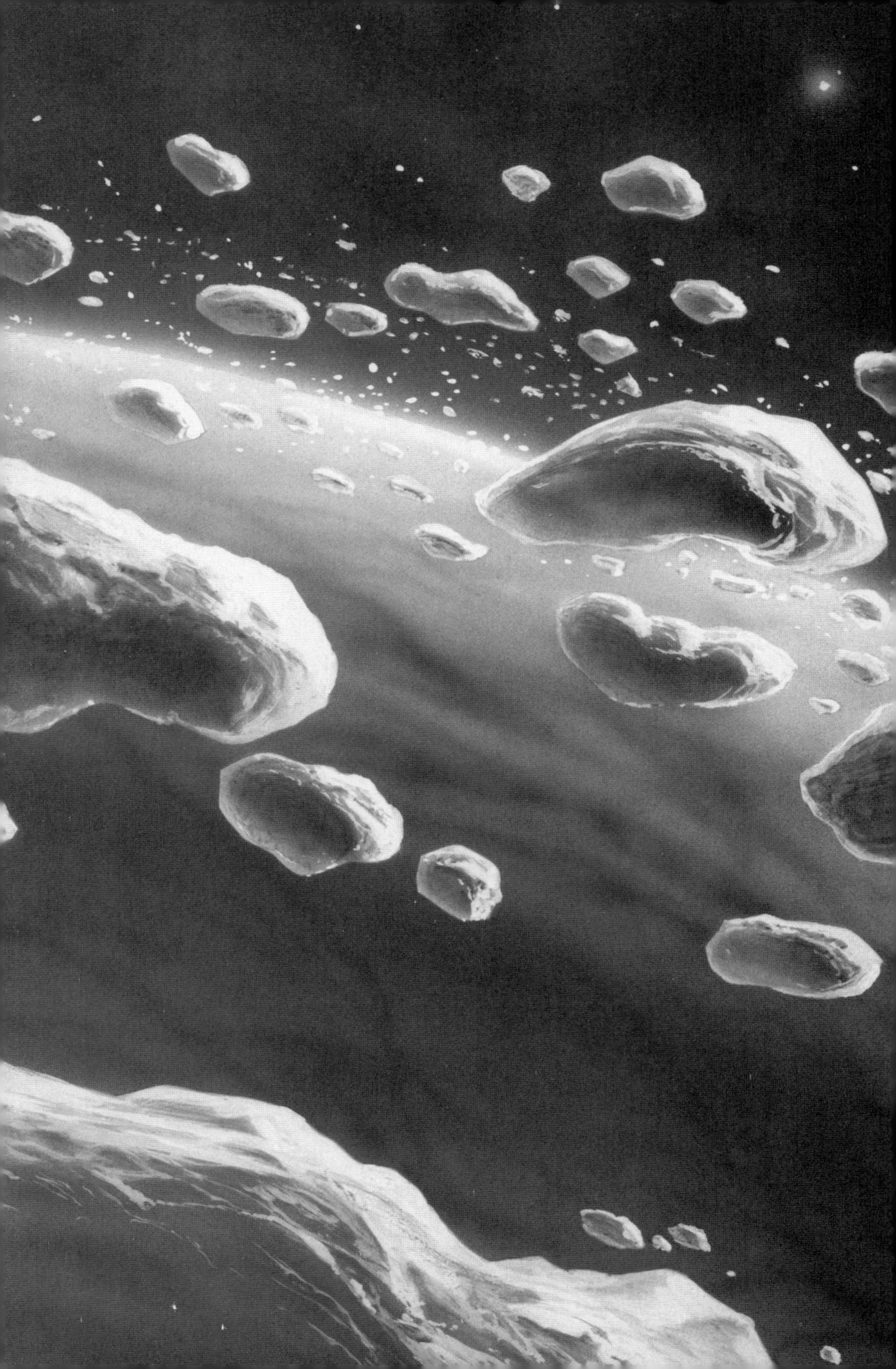

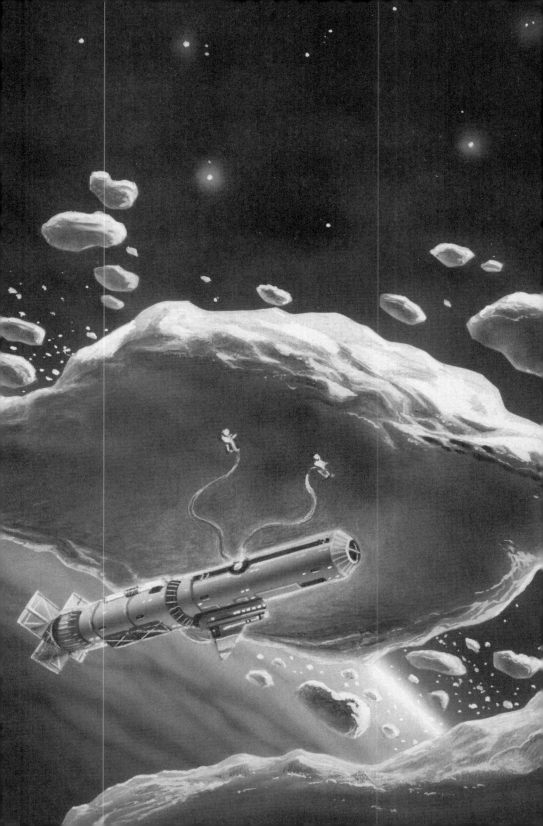

Tessa had seen asteroids before — many times, in fact — in her job as a space archaeologist. She had seen asteroid fields that were so densely packed that the great hunks of rock careened off each other constantly, like metal balls in her grandfather's ancient pinball machine. She had seen asteroids wandering alone in the black void, rocky adventurers off in search of a new place to settle. She had even seen an empty city, older than any civilization on Earth, built across a hundred asteroids that ringed a blue-white star, all the asteroids webbed together with strands of metal no thicker than a human hair.

In all her travels, though, Tessa had never seen such a wonder. For the asteroids that circled *this* world settled together in a layer that was only two hundred meters thick. It was so uniform and neat that it was unsettling.

Lenora Kelley, her partner on this particular space walk, called the planet Newton I, after her Great Uncle Newton. She had called the last planet Stacy II, after her sister, and the one before had been Charlie V, named after Len's best friend in high school. Tessa thought naming planets after friends and family was kind of silly, but it meant a lot to Len, so she let her do it.

In Tessa's mind, though, this planet was called "The World of a Thousand Moons." For that's what all these rocks were — tiny, spinning moons. She longed to see them from the planet's surface. I'll bet it looks like the sky is full of diamond dust, she thought with a dreamy smile. It must be beautiful.

Tessa glanced back at the silvery ship that floated a hundred meters away. She could just see her companion as she slipped off her rocket pack and prepared to push herself into the tiny maintenance hatch on the *Star Catcher*. Len had been chosen to come on this walk, not because she was an expert on asteroids, but because she was the ship's mechanic. The *Star Catcher's* main drive had been acting up, and Len hoped to fix it before they moved on to their next site.

Tessa felt a little sorry for Len. She had spent the last hour tethering Tessa to this particular asteroid, anchoring her three strong steel cables out to three distant points on the large rock — not easy work to be sure. And now she had to fix the ship's drive, a job that could take hours. But Tessa had to admit, she enjoyed the company. Space was lovely, but very, very empty.

Tessa touched a button and tightened one of the tethers, pulling herself closer to the groove before her. The cables allowed her to stay secured to the asteroid's surface and, at the same time, keep her hands free. By touching the controls at her waist, Tessa could adjust any or all of the tethers, taking up slack to hold her more securely, or letting it out so she could float free of the surface and change positions.

Len's head turned toward her. "Hey Tessa! You figured out what those grooves are yet?"

Tessa snorted. "I just started! I haven't got all the dust out of the first one yet."

Len's tiny silver figure moved as she secured her rocket pack to the magnetic clip beside the maintenance hatch.

She secured her own tether to a hook next to the hatch so she wouldn't float off into space, then popped the hatch open. The whole top half of her body disappeared as she shoved herself inside. Her voice, however, was still loud in Tessa's ear. "Well, hurry up. Darnel says we have to be out of here in 48 hours. Those supplies we picked up at Rigel have to be delivered to the Horus colony on schedule."

Tessa sighed, her disgust evident. She bent down over the deep groove that cut into the asteroid's surface. It wasn't a natural formation, she was sure of it. But she hadn't a clue as to what had made it. "I need 48 days to figure it out, Len, not 48 hours. You know that as well as I do."

Len grunted as she answered. She must be hard at work on the drive. "Yeah, well. Without the money we make off the supply runs, you'd never have a chance to figure out anything, now would you?"

Tessa didn't answer. She knew Len was right, but she didn't have to like it. Her soft-bristled brush uncovered an odd rock, and all thoughts of supplies and money flew from her mind in an instant. The rock was as large as her fist and as smooth and round as a river stone. Except there was no rushing water here in space to wear off the rough edges. Its surface was black with a slight metallic sheen. She wondered if it was iron, for that's what it looked most like. She wasn't a materials expert, so she couldn't be sure.

Picking up the stone with one hand, she brushed at the groove and uncovered another stone. And another.

26

She held the first one up, turning it this way and that. "Huh. That's weird..."

"What?" said Len.

"I found an unusual stone..." She trailed off as something moved to her right. Something glistening and blue. She whirled as fast as her tethers would allow. She watched as a blob of something resembling liquid turquoise drifted by. It spun slowly end over end as it moved out of the asteroid field in the direction of the ship.

She gasped in astonishment. "Len! Look at this!"

Len didn't respond right away. Tessa could hear her muttering in her headset. She watched as the blob floated farther away from her. She tried to judge where it was going. It looked as if it was headed for the middle of the ship. She felt her stomach knot in nervousness as she watched it roll along in a slow, almost graceful, arc. "Len ... you need to look at this."

Still no answer. The blob traveled a few more meters. Then she was sure where it was going. "Len!" she shouted into her mike. "You need to get out of there, NOW!"

Len gave a muffled protest and started to pull out of the hatch. It was a tight fit, and she looked like a worm wriggling out of an apple. "This better be important, Tessa. I just opened up the power unit."

The blob's progress wasn't fast, but it was relentless. On and on it tumbled. Tessa wasn't sure Len was going to make it in time. "Len, hurry! There's something coming your way! It's going to hit..."

Len's head popped out of the hatch and she turned. The blue blob was now only a few meters away from her and closing. Len gave a yelp of surprise and pushed off from the ship. She floated out into space until her tether stopped her motion. The blob hit the ship at the exact spot where Len had been working. Tessa expected it to rebound off the metal hull and spin out into space. To her horror and Len's, it didn't.

It stuck fast to the side of the ship. And it molded itself around the spot where Len's tether was anchored, and stayed there.

That one action set the blob apart from the other hunks of rock in the asteroid field. That action wasn't natural.

The thing looked like liquid, but didn't behave that way. A blob of liquid would have hit the side of the ship and rebounded, either still in one piece or in a myriad of spinning droplets. But it wouldn't have stuck like glue as this thing did.

For a long moment, neither of them said anything. Tessa could hear Len's heavy breathing in her ear. Her own breathing echoed harshly in her helmet.

Finally, Tessa could stand it no longer. "What's it doing, Len? What's happening?"

"It … it's doing something to my tether." Len's voice was tense. "I can't tell what." She twisted her body to get a better view. Her voice rose a notch. "I think it's eating through the cable. Tessa!"

Tessa gasped as Len's cable detached from the side of the *Star Catcher*, leaving Len floating free in space. Her tether stretched out in the direction of the ship, but it wouldn't do her any good now. Len's rocket pack, which could've maneuvered her back to the *Star Catcher*, was still fastened to the hull. Len had no way of getting back to safety. She was slowly drifting out into the asteroid field. Tessa would be of little or no help herself, since she was still fastened securely to the asteroid.

The worst part was, the blue blob hadn't stayed on the ship. It had stayed on the tether, and was now creeping along its length toward Len.

Tessa thumbed the switch on her helmet. "Darnel!" she called to their companion in the ship. "Darnel! We need help. Len's in trouble."

Darnel's deep voice filled her ear. "What kind of trouble, Tessa?"

Tessa quickly filled him in.

"It'll take me a few minutes to suit up, Tessa. Hang on."

Tessa watched the blue blob crawl along Len's cable. The steel disappeared into the thing and didn't come out on the other side. It seemed to be eating it...

"Len, release the cable from your suit."

Len's hands reached to do just that. After a moment, she said in a tight voice. "It's stuck, Tessa. I can't get it off."

Tessa blinked at her in disbelief. "You're kidding, right?" The blue creature, for that's what it must be, a *creature* and not a rock, had now eaten a third of the tether. Len was in real trouble.

"Of course I'm not kidding!" Len's tone bordered on complete panic. "Would I kid about something like that?"

Tessa's thoughts raced. "We need to cut it off..."

Len's voice brightened. "I have a cutter tool just inside the maintenance hatch. If I could get there." Tessa could see her head move as she looked around for something to push off of to make her way back to the ship. Unfortunately, the space around her was empty.

Len needed something to propel her back toward the *Star Catcher*. A push ... a shove ... a nudge from a neighboring rock. Anything. Tessa's brow furrowed in thought, her hand tightening around the smooth stone.

Suddenly, her eyes widened. The stone. Of course!

"Hang on, Len. I'm going to try something."

"Well, hurry up, would you? It's getting closer." Tessa could see that the creature was now halfway to Len — and seemed to be moving faster.

"All right. Be ready." Len hung directly between Tessa's position and the ship. She needed to push her toward it, and she could only think of one way. She lifted the rock in her hand, took careful aim, and threw it at Len's back with a throw that would have made her softball coach proud. The rock sailed like a missile through the empty space and hit Len squarely between the shoulders.

"Bull's-eye!" shouted Tessa.

Len grunted with the impact, but to her and Tessa's relief, she began drifting very slowly toward the ship. "Hey great, Tessa."

Tessa smiled and glanced at the creeping creature. Her expression of satisfaction quickly changed to one of concern. The creature was extending long pieces of itself, like tentacles, reaching along the length of the cable. One of the tentacles waved only about five meters from Len's helmeted face.

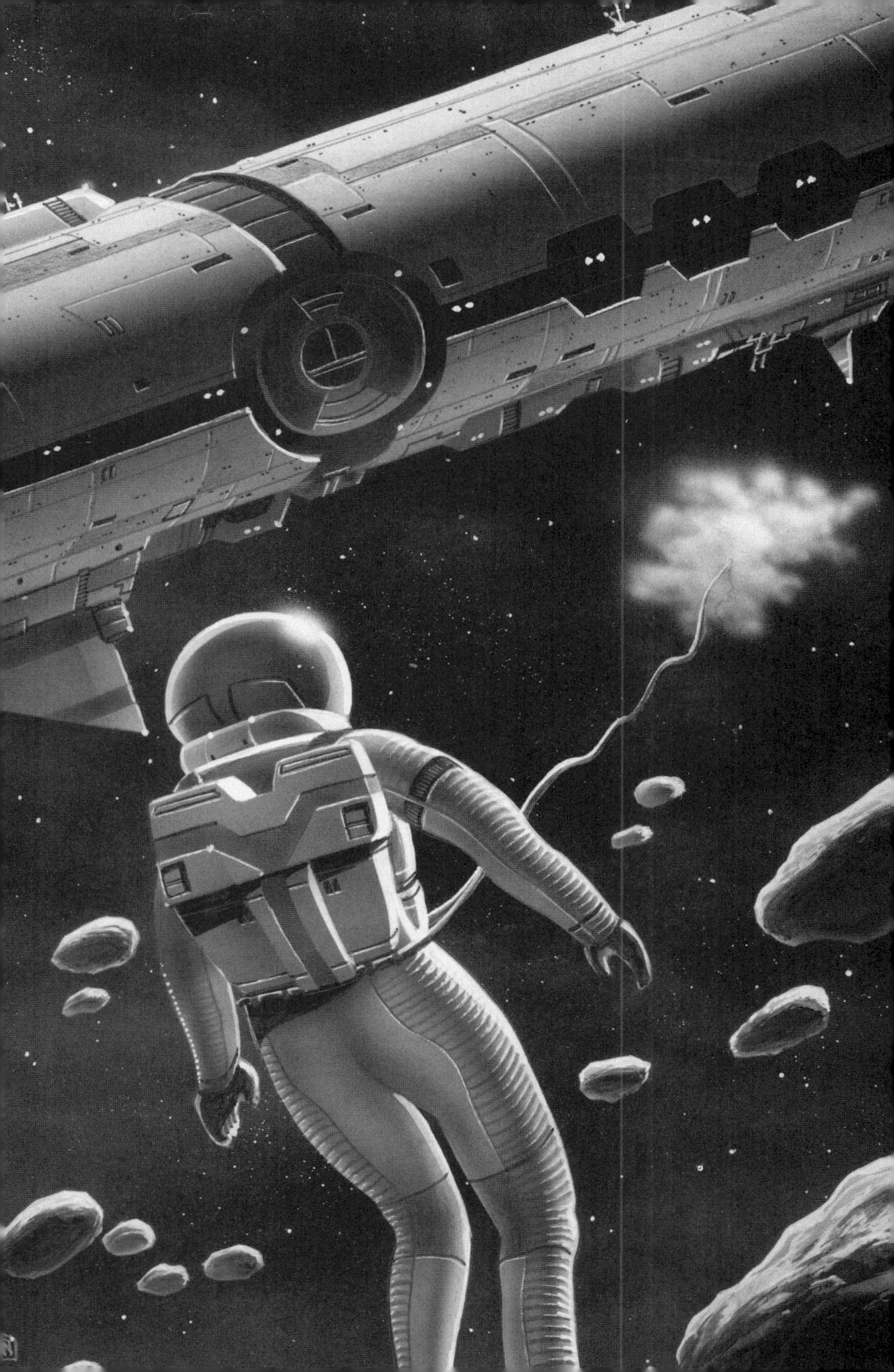

Len noticed the tentacle at the same time as Tessa. "Uh, Tess … can you speed me up any?" Her voice cracked on the last word.

Tessa wasted no time, snatching a second smooth stone from the asteroid's surface. She flung this one with all her might, hoping to give Len the biggest shove she could, at the same time hoping her suit would withstand the impact without damage. The rock hit her on her left arm, shifting her angle slightly, but still pushing her toward the ship. Her speed increased considerably.

In less than ten seconds, Len bumped into the *Star Catcher's* hull and grabbed hold. She pulled herself to the maintenance hatch by means of handgrips placed in the slick metal surface for just such a purpose, and quickly reached inside. The blue creature was pulled along with her, still reaching with its probing tentacles. Len's cutter sliced the cable at the exact moment the long tentacle touched her helmet. She yelled and frantically shoved the cable. It flew away from the ship, off into space.

The creature, still clinging to the steel thread, had no choice but to go with it.

Tessa let out the breath she had been holding as the cable and creature drifted away from Len. She could hear Len's shaky breathing in her helmet headset. "You okay, Len?"

"Yeah." She waved toward her. "Thanks."

"You're welcome," said Tessa, still eyeing the blue creature. As she watched, it gently pulled the last of the tether into its body, where it disappeared. Then the creature pulled back into its original, round shape. It kept on drifting until it neared a small asteroid. To Tessa's astonishment, it reached out a thin tentacle, touched the asteroid — and gently pushed itself off.

Tessa gasped in alarm. The thing was now heading straight for her. And it was coming fast.

"Tessa!" yelled Len. She fumbled with her rocket pack, trying to slip the thing on while still holding on to the ship. "I'm coming!"

Tessa stared at the creature as its glossy, blue surface pulsed and throbbed closer to her. Even if Len got her pack on, she would be too late. She shot a look at the ship's main hatch. Darnel was nowhere in sight. Tessa was on her own.

She bent and picked up a third stone, and felt around with probing fingers until she found a fourth, then a fifth. She straightened and took aim at the creature's center. "This worked before," she muttered under her breath. "It'd better work again."

She pitched the stone hard. It hit the creature exactly where she had been aiming. But, instead of bouncing off the creature's surface, the stone was sucked in, like it had hit quicksand. It was eating the rocks too, thought Tessa absently. Amazing.

But to Tessa's relief, the creature's speed slowed considerably. She took another stone and heaved it as she had the first.

The creature sucked this one up too, and stopped almost dead in space. Across the void, Len whooped.

"You did it, Tessa!"

Tessa grinned in satisfaction and let go with the third rock. "Get out of here, you stupid thing! We're not going to be your dinner." The rock hit to one side, almost glancing off the slippery-looking surface, but the thing managed to hold on and engulf it in folds of turquoise flesh. The momentum from the throw pushed the creature off toward a cluster of smaller, more distant asteroids.

Then Len was by her side. Tessa unfastened her tethers and grabbed hold of the mechanic's arm. A burst from Len's rocket pack and in short order, they were back at the ship. Tessa kept hold of Len as Len snatched a handgrip. Both turned to watch the bright blue creature.

It reached the smaller asteroids, touched off with a tentacle, and started in the direction of the spinning world below them. It touched off again and again, gaining speed each time. Soon, gravity would take hold, and it would fall into the wispy white clouds that raced through the planet's thin atmosphere.

"It's heading toward the surface," said Tessa. "I wonder..." She scanned the area, and by looking carefully, she could see three other pinpoints of blue that could only be more of the creatures. One looked to be going down toward the planet, but two seemed to be rising toward the asteroids. A faint, wispy tail of white trailed behind each, just like the exhaust that flowed out of Len's rocket pack.

"Well, I'll be..." said Len. "They have some sort of propulsion."

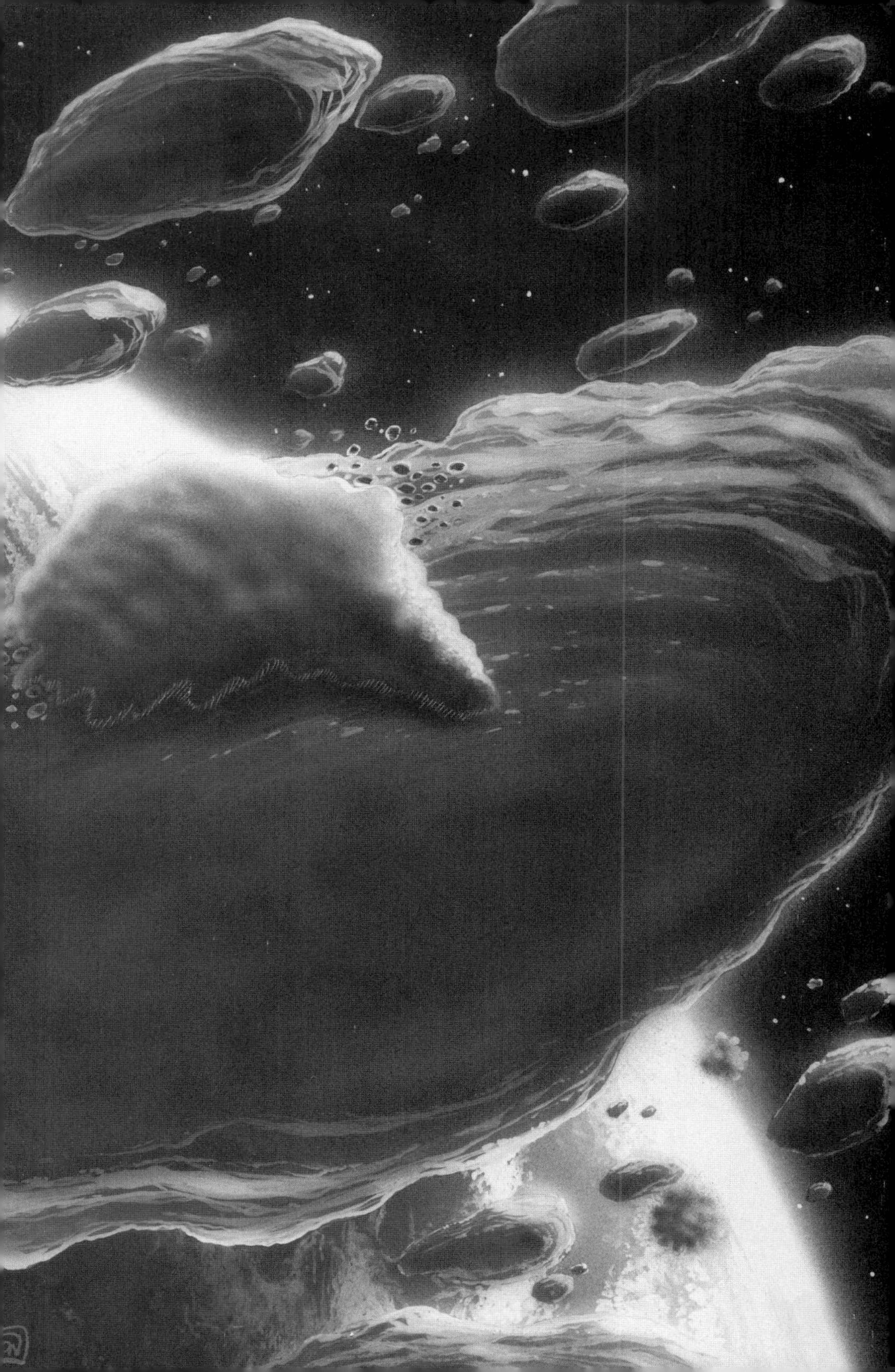

Tessa nodded, smiling in wonderment. "Yeah. Instead of diving down into their ocean, it's like they're diving up into space."

Len considered that. "To eat, do you think?"

Tessa remembered the smooth rocks with their metallic surfaces. It had sucked those in as eagerly as it had eaten Len's cable. "Yeah, I think it eats those smooth stones I found." She frowned. "But it didn't do anything to the asteroids it pushed off from. That still doesn't explain the grooves. And I don't know what those stones *are*. They're strange..."

Len's hand came into view, her pointing finger trembling. "Look!"

Tessa followed her finger. A large asteroid spun slowly in front of them, revealing what had been on the other side. Clinging to its surface was a great pink glob of pulsating goo. The wide body of the thing narrowed at one end to a hard, round knot. The end of the knot was pushing along the asteroid's surface. Behind the glob, a deep groove trailed away to the asteroid's horizon.

"That thing is grazing on the asteroid like a cow on grass!" Tessa's mouth fell open and she blinked. "It's eating the rock!" She heard Len chuckle.

"And look what's coming out along its sides," Len said. Tessa squinted. Along the creature's pulsating sides, bits of shiny, smooth rock emerged, some to drift off into space, some to settle gently on the asteroid's surface. Tessa now realized what the smooth stones she had found were. And what the blue creature had been eating.

"Eeww! Gross!" She wiped her gloved hand on her thigh in disgust. "That stuff is…"

At the moment, the main hatch popped open and Darnel shot out into space with a burst from his rocket pack. "What? What stuff? What's going on?"

Darnel's dramatic entrance broke the spell. Len laughed. Tessa found herself giggling. "We'll tell you inside, okay?" said Tessa. "And you really need to work on suiting up just a bit faster, Darnel."

"Hey!" said Darnel. "I got here, didn't I? What more do you want?" He frowned at them. His rocket pack gave another series of bursts, and he turned back toward the ship. "All that trouble," he mumbled. "And all they do is give me a hard time." He disappeared into the hatch.

Len sighed and guided Tessa toward the hatch. "You know," she said, "I'm thinking of changing the name of this place. How about we call it Edna I, after my aunt. She raised cattle, you see, and when I was at her house, I was always stepping in cow patties in the pasture…"

Tessa rolled her eyes and sighed as they left the asteroid pasture and entered the ship.

Dragonfly

by Mark Canter

Ket opened her eyes, still groggy from the blow, and screamed so long and loud that she fogged the faceplate of her helmet.

If not for her Expedition Suit, the dragon's attack would have torn through Ket's spine. Instead, the beast's scythe-like pincers had struck between Ket's shoulders and snagged Rebreather, the air-recycling unit. From the corners of her eyes Ket watched vapor spewing from punctures in Rebreather's lungs, forming white puffs in the air like her own icy breath on a warm morning. Ket imagined she heard a gurgling wheeze as Rebreather struggled to heal its wounds. But the dragon's giant buzzing wings drowned out all sound and pummeled Ket with vibrations that numbed her to the bone.

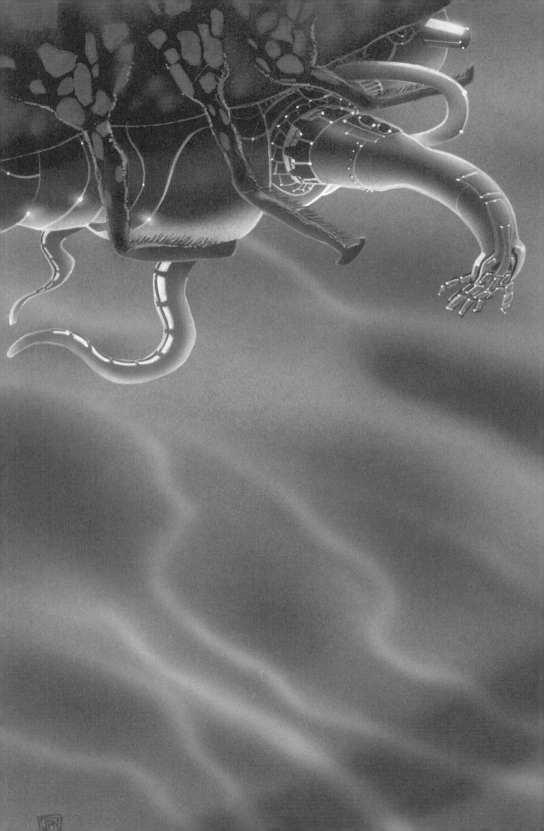

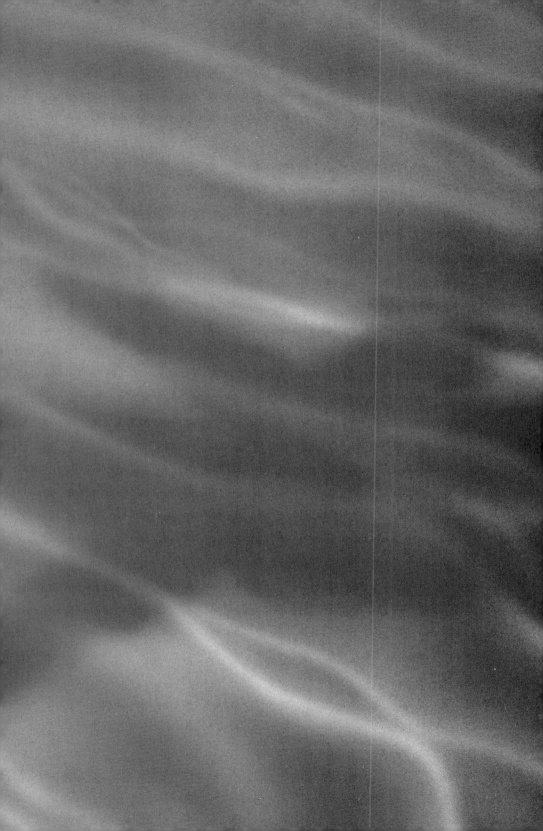

Far below, froth splashed and heaved on the surface of an alien sea. Most of the world was covered with salt water. The native sentient species called the planet Earth, but only because they were land dwellers, Ket thought. It would be much more fitting to call the planet Ocean. But then, Ket and her kind dwelled under permanent ice on an ocean-covered moon, so she was partial to oceans. In Earth's heavy gravity, the waves crawled like pale green worms over the darker green surface of the sea.

Ket had only glimpsed what hit her. Now she twisted and craned her neck against the windblast from blurring wings to get a better look at the hunter that was carrying her off as its prey. What she saw made her hearts hammer a duet. She breathed out slowly and evenly to quiet her terror.

Don't panic is the first rule of any emergency. How many times had the Queen-Explorer told Ket and the other Sister-Explorers that?

"Faceplate, de-fog," Ket whistled to Suit, producing shrill notes from inside a gas-filled sinus in her skull.

The visor cleared. "Suit, drop my body temperature twenty degrees," she whistled, and felt an instant icy chill surge through her bloodstream. No time to enjoy the pleasure.

Okay, Ket, what have you got yourself into this time? Fourteen expeditions to Earth, and most of them had put her in danger from the local life-forms. That was the risk of studying megafauna, the giant creatures that dwarfed Ket. Even so, this was her first emergency on Earth that might really get her killed.

The droning wings were shaking Ket dizzy. The predator was definitely a dragon of some kind. Six legs, three body parts: head, thorax, abdomen. This particular species had a long, cylindrical body, with a double set of wings on each side. Each sphere of its twin eyes seemed half as big as the Survey Ship Ket had arrived in. But while Ket's Ship was covered with dull gray scales, the dragon's faceted eyes reflected a bright spectrum of colors.

The four long, transparent wings identified this species. Ket had seen its kind before on a holo. What was the native name for it?

"Dragonfly," she spoke aloud, making the feathery, purple coil of her tongue imitate the harsh language of the dominant species of this titanic world. Then she whistled in her own musical language, "Suit, show data on dragonflies."

A holo popped up and hovered in the top left corner of her helmet, slowly rotating through each of three axes. Even in the holo the dragon's big eyes glowed iridescently. No more information was available.

Well, that's what science expeditions are for, aren't they? And that's why I became a xenozoologist, Ket thought. If I live through this, I'll have some interesting facts to add to the knowledge of dragonflies.

Ket spread the fan of skin flaps on her scalp and let Suit chill the many tiny blood vessels that cooled her brain. It felt icy and good. She tried to keep breathing slowly, deeply, to stay calm. But Ket noticed it was getting harder to breathe at all, let alone deeply. Evidently, Rebreather had not been able to heal itself.

"Trillion," Ket whistled, addressing a swarm of nanobots that lived in Suit's bloodstream. "Rebreather repair. Priority one." Ket imagined another sound from Rebreather, this time a sigh of relief, as a team of microscopic robots flowed into its bloodstream from Suit's immune system to help Rebreather restore its injured flesh.

The dragonfly rose higher on buzzing wings, carrying Ket toward a red clay cliff. Perhaps to a nesting place to feed its young, Ket thought, sickly. Or would it deposit eggs in Ket's body, so that when the dragon larvae hatched they would have lunch, living and warm?

Interesting facts to add to the knowledge of dragonflies.

Ket had not worn a force-field generator because the so-called "portable" unit was too heavy and clumsy to lug around on her back in Earth's high gravity. Without the protective field, the dragon could easily tear through Ket's Expedition Suit with those huge mandibles that fed its cavernous mouth. Suddenly Ket remembered herself in larval form, ripping through crimson bubbles in the ice to devour the squirming life inside. She shuddered. She had to escape.

Of course, to kill the flying dragon now would mean plummeting to her own death. She must wait until they had arrived wherever they were heading; to the red cliff, it seemed.

Ket got ready to fight. The dragonfly's attack had broken both of Ket's tentacle arms; they flopped uselessly inside long, thin sleeves, as Trillion devoted itself to repairing Rebreather. But her abdominal claspers remained undamaged. It took only a moment longer with the shorter arms to unsnap a laser drill from its holster. Ket raised the tool in front of her faceplate: "Drill, on," she whistled. "Setting, maximum." A green light winked on at the base of the tool; a second light flashed red, showing the drill's power was set to penetrate diamond.

The red cliff loomed large, filling Ket's faceplate.

Breathing had become hard work. Ket felt overheated, in spite of the ice crystals that had formed on her scalp flaps. Rebreather was near death. If Rebreather died, so would Ket, and she knew Suit could not reanimate her for more than a few minutes, not long enough for Ket to make it back to Ship. So Ket would die, again. Then Suit would automatically switch to stasis mode, keeping Ket's body in frozen suspension, awaiting rescue and reanimation at a proper medical facility. But in that vulnerable state, the dragonfly would surely eat her, or something more hideous.

"If I should stop breathing," Ket whistled to Suit in a rapidfire melody, "do not reanimate me and do not place me in stasis."

"Are you sure you don't want to reanimate, Ket?"

Ket flinched. It was so rare for Suit to whistle back to her that it always came as a surprise. The fact that it communicated to Ket in the Queen-Explorer's signature whistle did not lessen the shock.

"I repeat," Ket whistled, "If I die, do *not* reanimate me. Do *not* place me in stasis. Disgorge my body and leave it behind. If you manage to somehow escape the dragon, place yourself in long-term standby mode to await rescue. Good luck," Ket whistled. "And may you be inhabited again and again."

"And may you be animated again and again," Suit whistled back, in the Queen's high, trilling notes.

The dragonfly glided down toward the red cliff's edge. Ket readied herself, gripping the laser drill in her central clasper. "Laser, on," Ket whistled. A blue beam shot out from the tool. The black dragon alighted on the bluff overlooking the sea. As soon as it touched down, Ket swiveled underneath and stabbed the blue laser beam into a giant eye. She stirred the cutting light around and around inside the wound, scrambling and frying the dragon's brain in the same motion.

The dragonfly's head jerked in crazy loops, as if trying to flee the fire twirling inside its brain. Its wings went still. Then its full weight crashed down on top of Ket.

Ket's scalp flaps drooped with relief. At least *that* part of my nightmare is over, she thought. Then the sizzling hole in the dragon's eye spilled its contents. A thick, yellow jelly rained down on Ket in hot, splashing globs. For a long moment she fought down the urge to be sick. Fog on her faceplate was bad enough.

With Suit's help, Ket managed to wriggle out from under the dragonfly. She stood back and stared at the animal, long and black and sleek, with wings the size of an aircraft.

Inspiration struck.

Ket began to see how she might get back to Ship on the other side of the water. But she was forced to breathe faster now, and her body temperature kept creeping upward.

She had very little time to make her plan work.

As Ket set about preparing to escape, she thought grimly that her predicament seemed like a horror version of a game she had played as a larva, called "Fortunately/ Unfortunately."

Fortunately, when the dragon had swooped down from behind and plucked Ket off the ground, its pincers had missed Ket's spine and stabbed Rebreather instead.

Unfortunately, Rebreather was so badly wounded that even the combined effort of Trillion could save only part of one lung. Rebreather was losing its ability to recycle Ket's outbreaths into breathable air.

Fortunately, this planet had enough mass to hold onto a thick atmosphere. *Unfortunately,* Earth's atmosphere was so toxic to Ket, that just breathing it would make her burst into flames.

Fortunately, Ket wasn't planning to breathe the air. She only wanted to use it to fly back to Ship. *Unfortunately,* she didn't have an aircraft to fly.

Fortunately, she did have one huge, dead dragon. Which, Ket remembered, had smoothly glided down to a landing. From this tall cliff, the dead dragon could serve as Ket's glider, to fly her back over the finger of sea to the low, salt marsh where Ship waited.

47

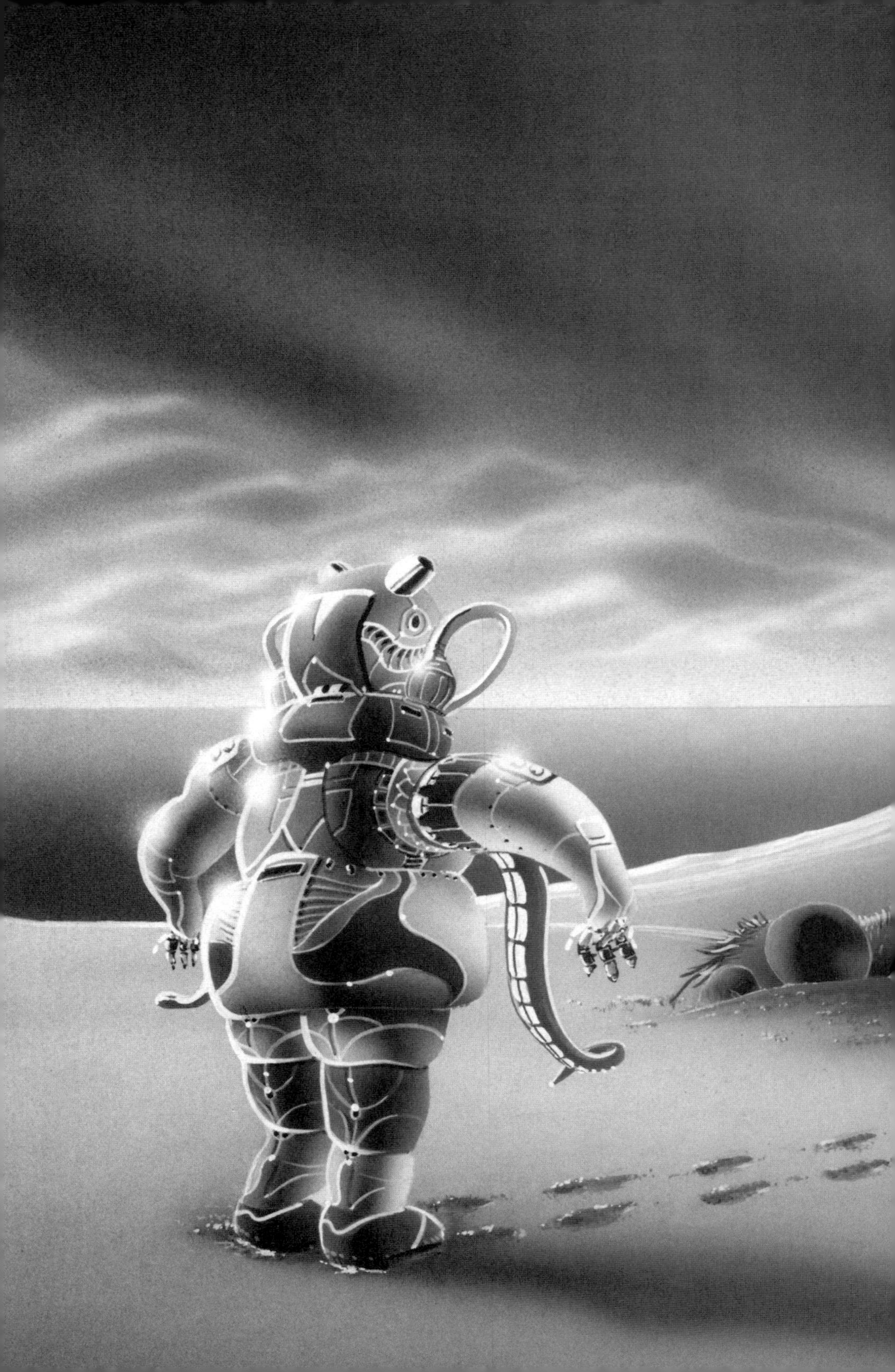

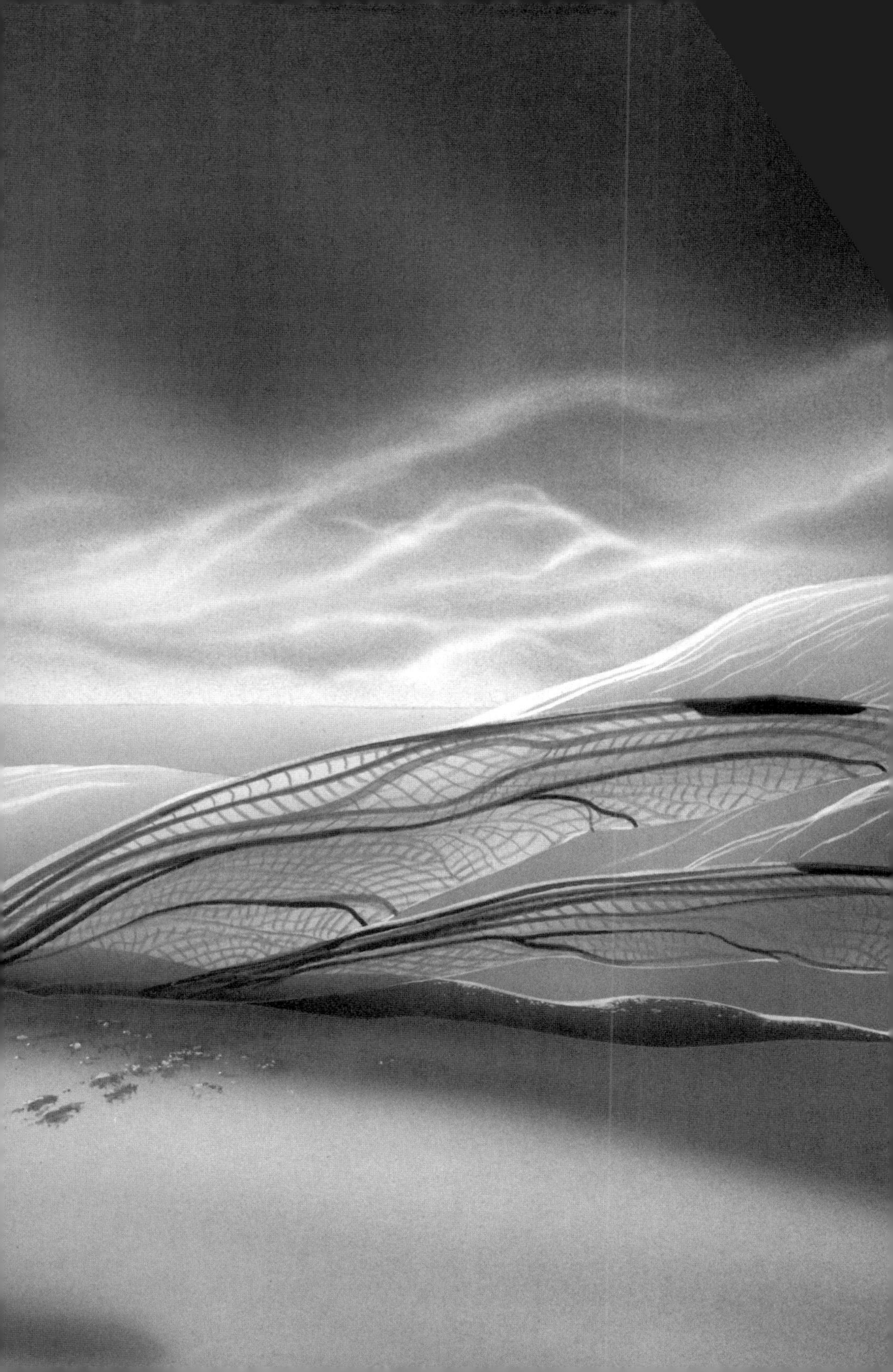

Unfortunately, Ket didn't remember much from Explorer Seminary about aerodynamic theory — at the time, it had seemed obsolete to her. Survey Ships traveled in the vacuum of space, where the study of bodies moving through air did not apply, or they traveled on-planet by repelling gravity waves. So Ket had no idea whether her flight plan was ingenious or suicidal.

Fortunately, she had no idea whether her flight plan was ingenious or suicidal. Because if she were convinced her strategy was impossible — rather than just desperate — she would be stranded on this alien crag, without hope, dying.

With Suit's help, Ket aligned the dragonfly's wings and gave them positive dihedral — a V-shaped upward tilt — for stability during flight. She straightened out the dragon's slender body and then sprayed the entire airframe — wings and fuselage — with a thin film of liquid titanium from her kit. A moment later, she tapped a wing with the spray gun, testing for hardness; the shiny silver clinked metallically.

Dragonflies were not equipped with ailerons, elevator, or rudder for flight control, so Ket would have to bank and steer the big kite by shifting her body weight, as in the sport Earthlings called hang-gliding.

Riding beneath the glider in the right spot was critical, Ket knew, or the aircraft's center of gravity would be skewed, causing an unbalanced and uncontrollable flight. Sucking in and holding her breath, Ket detached herself from Rebreather and used glue-rivets to fasten the dragonfly's legs to Rebreather in the same place they had grasped it before. Then she backed beneath the outstretched dragon wings, recoupled her lungs to Rebreather, and gasped for air.

"Suit, maximum cold," Ket whistled, "and inject strength hormones, all you've got left."

"What about reserves?" Suit whistled.

"Keep no reserves. Give me everything, now. Chill me down."

A flood of icy energy surged through Ket's blood, into her muscles and lit up her brain in a white, frosty light. Only her Explorer's training kept her from fainting in the freezing ecstasy.

Ket gathered her physical might and stood up, lifting the giant dragonfly glider over her bent back. She gazed down from the crest of a slope that led to the cliff and the sheer drop to the sea.

She stared at the edge where the world ended and the sky began.

Everything was ready. But Ket was too scared to budge. A fall from this height would smash her against the water. Then the pale green waves would crawl over her like worms and gulp her down.

Ket was about to tell Suit to go to standby, to reabsorb the energy nutrients from Ket's bloodstream before they were wasted.

Then the Queen-Explorer's unmistakable melody whistled to Ket.

"Dear one," the warbling said, "when I was uploaded into Suits for all my Sister-Explorers, it was so they could inhabit me, as my genes and my teachings inhabit all of you. Now I tell you that I am proud of you, Ket. But an Explorer must *return*, to report on the wonders she has found."

Ket sighed. Snowflakes of love fell from her eye stalks and a glacial blue oil oozed from trembling gills.

Ket decided.

She hefted the dragonfly and ran down the slope into the wind rising from the sea. The airflow over the dragonfly's wings gave lift and tugged Ket's feet off the ground. She flattened her body into a prone position as she floated beyond the cliff's edge. Red clay plunged to green sea.

Ket was flying. Dragonflying over the wrinkling waves.

The dragonfly glider flew well. Too well. After a few scary and glorious moments, Ket was more than half way to the far shore and she gazed below at the green marsh grasses. But she couldn't bring the glider down. She was caught in a thermal — a rising column of heated air — that was carrying her up and up, toward the fat underbelly of a summer cloud.

Ket tried to think of everything she knew about how airplanes fly. She recalled that flight involves the interplay of four forces: lift, weight, drag, and ... she couldn't remember the fourth one. Lift and — *whatever* — made a plane fly higher; and the other two forces — weight and drag — made a plane come down. Obviously, she could not increase her weight, but if she could increase drag, she should start to descend.

Ket lowered her body until it faced flat into the slipstream. The air buffeted against her, braking her forward movement. It worked. The glider started to drop. Now the green shore loomed close, filling Ket's faceplate, as the red cliff had done before.

But the whitecaps came rushing up fast. The spray reached for her feet as she shifted back into a more streamlined pose, but it was too late, she was going to hit the waves.

Suddenly, she remembered the other component of flight. *Thrust.* Of course! Thrust helped a plane fly higher. And Ket's Expedition Suit was equipped with steerable hydrogen jets for maneuvering outside Ship in space.

Ket whistled piercingly, "Suit, aft-thrusters, full power, NOW!"

Ka-whooosh. The kick of acceleration felt like being blasted from a sea-geyser. The glider shot up over the waves. Now, only waving grasses rushed by below.

"Thrusters, OFF!"

The dragonfly glider floated down smoothly to land on the soft marsh.

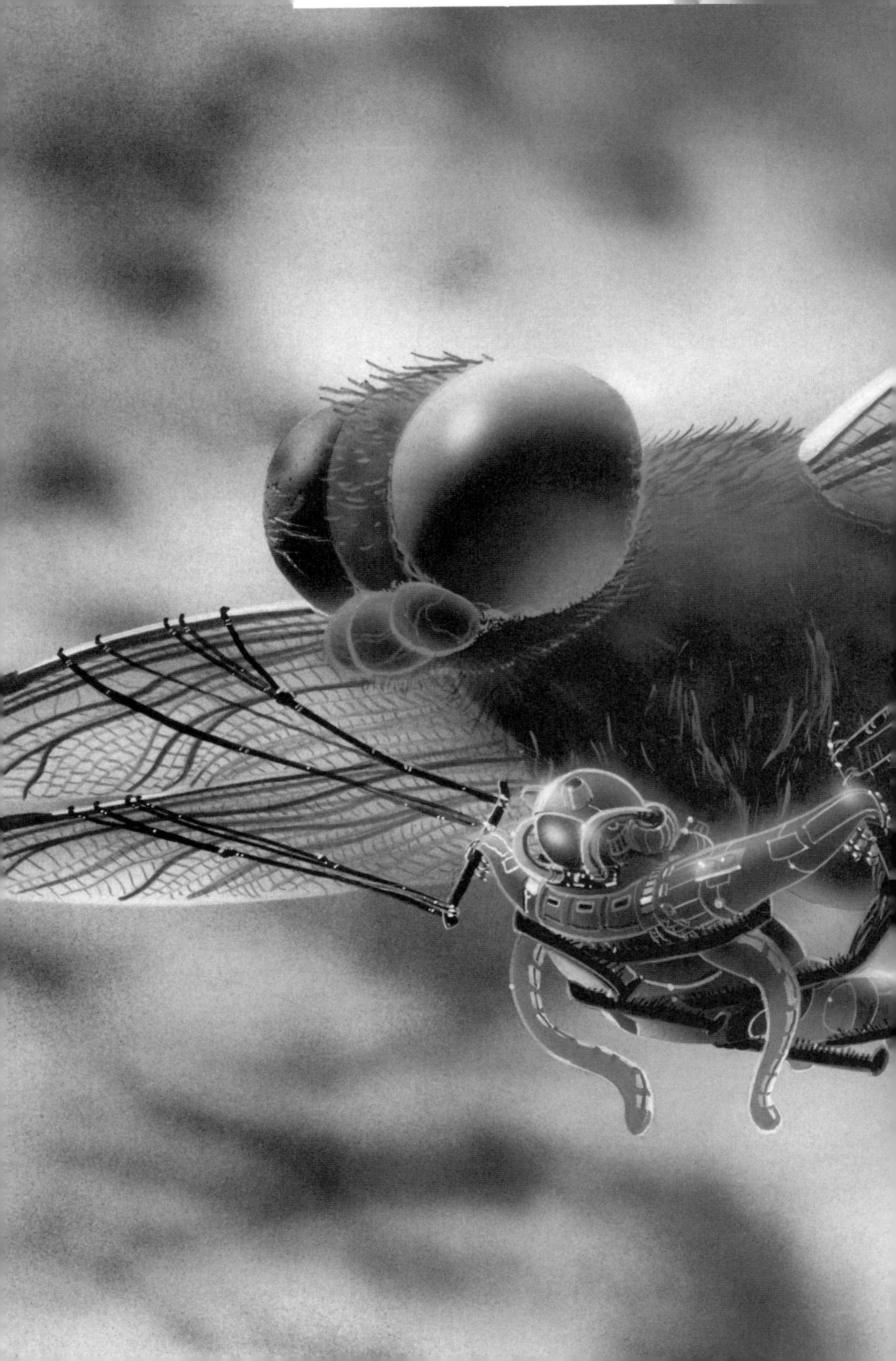

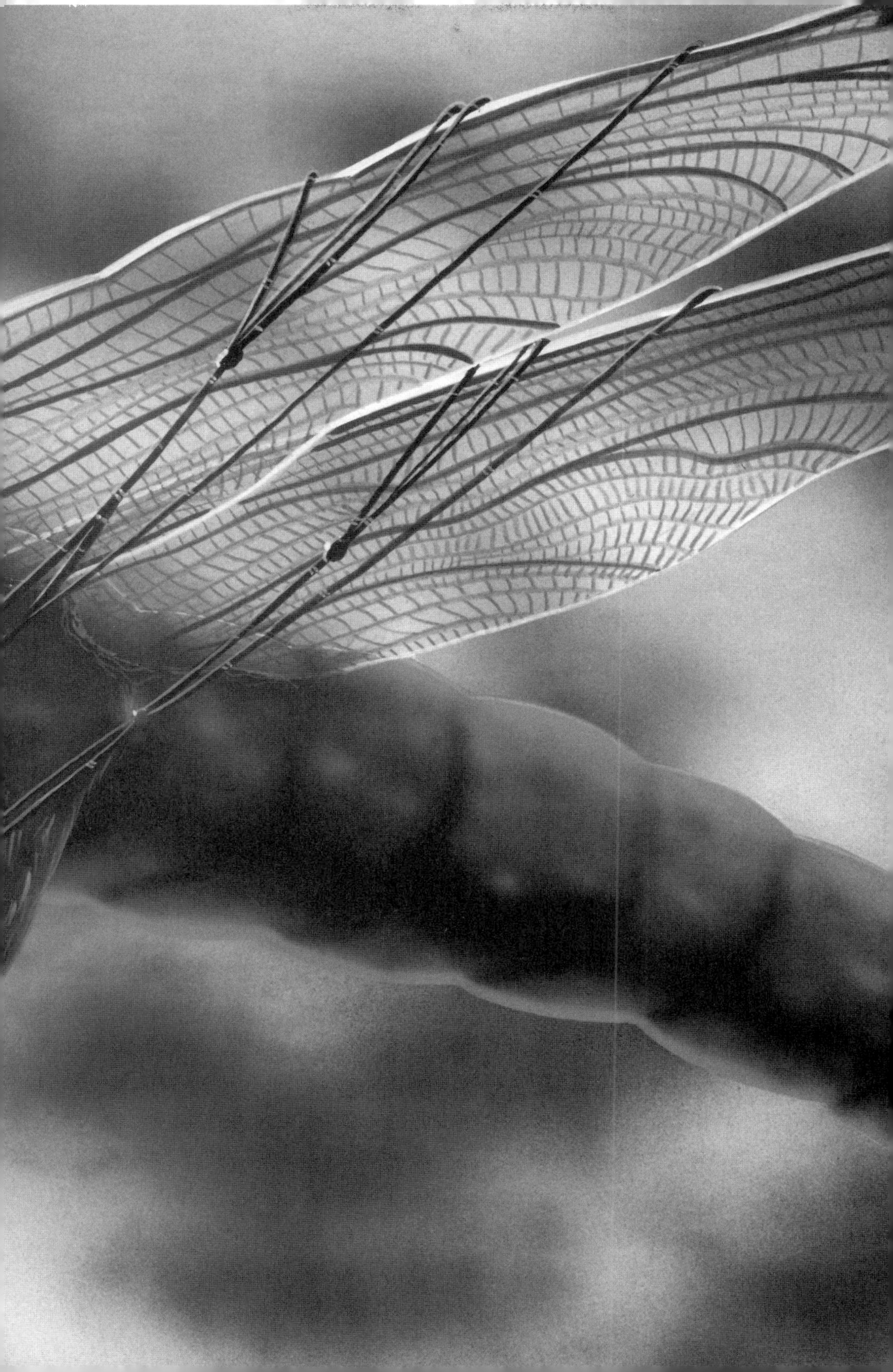

Back inside the freezing safety of Ship, Ket slept through a whole cycle in a tank of salt water, beneath an icecap. Suit rested in its recharging chamber. Rebreather sprouted lung buds in a slow whirlpool of pink slush.

When Ket awakened, she skittered straight to the lab. She plunked a specimen of the dragonfly into an enzyme bath and fed the digested flesh to Ship.

Ship tasted the dragonfly's genetic instructions and began to grow a virtual dragonfly in the space in front of Ket's head. Molecules clumped and folded and twisted into proteins, that linked in complex chains, that took on the structure of cells, that developed into tissues, that formed organs. In a moment, a scale holomodel of the dragonfly hovered in the middle of the room.

An ice fog wafted up from the deck and wet the feathery tips of Ket's tentacles as she began the virtual dissection. According to how she probed, the dragonfly's anatomy rotated in space, enlarged by magnitudes, vanished layer-by-layer. Ship recorded her findings. Ket tweeted and chittered, enjoying the work, her scalp-flaps coated with frost.

When she had finished the project, Ket telescoped her tentacles back into their sockets, and reflected on all she had learned.

"Giant dragons," she trilled to herself softly. "What a planet!"

In spite of its crushing gravity, deathly heat, and combustible atmosphere, Ket considered Earth beautiful — even bewitching — and studying its weird, enormous life-forms was worth the dangers.

She gazed with pride around the pearly interior curves of Ship. Every object glowed in her cool ultraviolet light. Ket could not imagine a life more rewarding than to be a scientist in the Order of Sister-Explorers.

Tether

by Jean-Louis Trudel

Life in space could be boring at the best of times. And sharing a shift in Blue 6 with an Earth girl threatened to be unspeakably boring.

Yet, once Ron finished resetting the radiation counters and the force gauges, there was nothing left to do but talk. Unless an emergency call came in, it was that or spend all shift peering out the porthole at the ungainly shapes of Space City.

Sure, they were there to keep an eye on the monitors, and the dust count, and the space debris simulations, but the computer did almost as good a job. The young pilot leaned back to strap himself into the couch of the emergency module, code-named Blue 6. He then turned toward his partner who was happily settled in the first aid alcove.

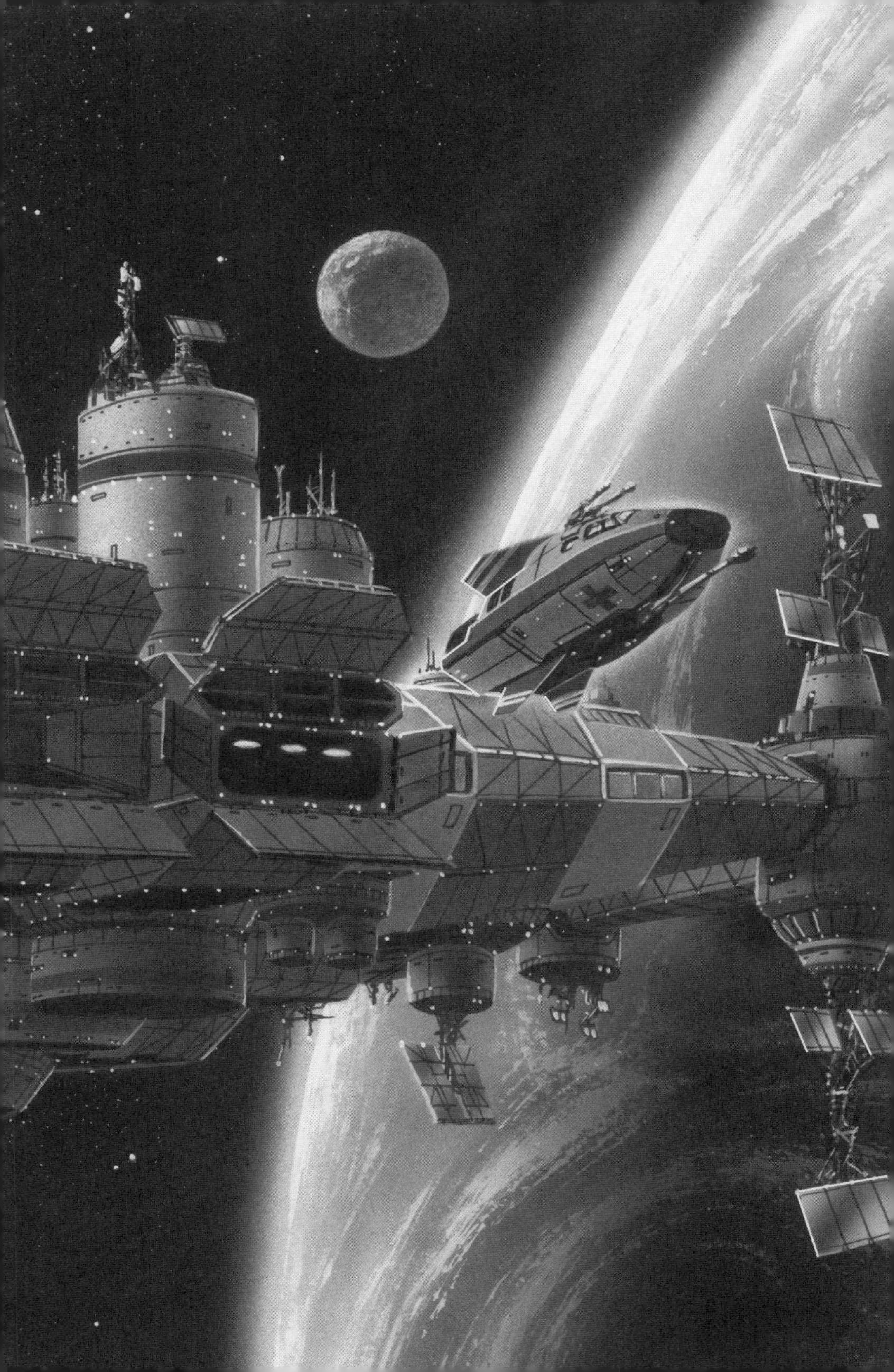

"So, Roz, what will you do with your bonus?"

Actually, for an Earth girl, she was all right, though Ron wasn't going to tell her that quite yet. Earlier, they had shared an embarrassed laugh when the truth had come out that Roz was short for Rosalind and Ron's full name was Oberon! Both of them had been named after Solar System moons, during a brief craze for astronomical names that had turned their parents' generation into blithering idiots. Roz had quite won him over by pointing out that it could have been worse — she might have been called Pandora or Desdemona, and he might have been named Janus!

Still, he intended to enjoy bossing her around for a couple more shifts, because she was junior and because he liked playing the role of the old space hand.

"You first," she replied.

"Me? Dust racers, Roz, that's what I'm going to spend the extra money on. I've got my eye on the upgraded model with solid-fuel boosters. Just what I need to tackle the new track on the Sea of Storms."

"Aren't those dangerous? Last year, there must have been over a dozen fatalities during the racing season."

"It's all part of the fun, Roz. Lunar gravity is so weak there's always plenty of time to bail out before a crash."

"But you could be killed!"

He shook his head. She was from Earth. Dirtside, the old-timers called it. And he was Moon-born. She would never understand the attraction of dust racing on the Moon. The racers were like giant spiders, with wheels at the end of extended metal legs, and the vehicles skittered wildly over the dust-covered slopes when the rocket units were

61

switched on. Sure, they crashed from time to time and a
torn vacsuit could be deadly. But learning how to handle
the ejection seat was the mark of the true racer pilot.

"Fun?" she repeated. "Well, if you say so. But I'll take
my bonus and put it in the bank. I'm saving to buy a
house in Siberia."

"A house! Isn't seventeen a bit young to think of
settling down?"

At the venerable age of nineteen, he certainly enter-
tained no such thoughts. She shook her head reprovingly:
"Buying any kind of property on Earth is very expensive,
Ron. If I don't start to save now, I'll never manage it."

"You're only up here for the money, then?"

The orbital work bonus was a sizable one for Earth
specialists, who found it hard to maintain their original
fitness level while living in weightlessness.

"Well, it was on my school's list of final year work
experiences. It sounded more fun than learning about
water purification in the Balkans..."

"I hear a distinct lack of enthusiasm," he challenged her.

"Oh, I like it up here, Ron, but..."

She didn't get a chance to finish. The main screen
came to life. The blurry image of a man's head appeared
in a video frame. His voice cut through the background
hiss of the open radio link.

"Medical emergency, medical em..." The man gasped.
"Is someone there? I've got trouble. Can you hear me?"

"Rosalind Pei here, aboard Blue 6. I'm the medic on
shift. What's the problem?"

The young woman was staring intently at the monitor,

as if she could tell from the image alone what the man's problem was.

"Heart attack, I think," the man said, wheezing. "Trouble breathing. Shooting pains in my... Please help! I'm on the supply run to the Hawking Observatory."

"I've got you," Ron said, locating the origin of the call. "We'll be there as quickly as possible."

He gunned the module's engines. Blue 6 slowly moved away from the ramshackle outbuildings of Space City, which had grown like mad since its humble beginnings as the International Space Station. The automated observatories were in neighbouring orbits, so that supplies could be easily ferried back and forth.

Ron smiled. Sometimes, life in space wasn't so boring...

The supply ship grew in Ron's screens as Blue 6 approached it. It was twice as long as the emergency module. The pilot's minuscule cockpit was lodged between the forward hold and the aft engines.

Ron handled the rendezvous, but it was Rosalind who left the module. She brought back the other pilot, partly tugging, partly pushing him through the connecting airlocks.

"How is he?" Ron called out, unwilling to look away from the controls.

"Heart failure; no doubt about it," she responded, too busy to say any more.

Life in orbit was not kind to people with incipient heart conditions. In free fall, the heart got used to minimal effort, especially if visitors from Earth stinted on their daily exercise. As a result, any unexpected physical strain could make a heart burst.

The pilot was half-unconscious when Rosalind strapped him into a life-support unit. He was an older man, with loose flesh on his arms and thinning blond hair. An old NASA badge on his uniform showed that he'd flown aboard the original Space Shuttles.

Ron watched through a small rearview mirror. Roz was an excellent medic for her age, and she was clearly determined to save the man's life. Her moves were smooth and practiced as she plugged in the pacemaker, hooked an oxygen feed to the man's nose, stuck probes into the skin over the failing heart...

His attention captured by the ongoing drama, Ron was taken by surprise when a loud bang echoed inside Blue 6. For a moment, his eyes unfocused. He shook his head, stunned. His ears were ringing, as if he'd been standing within a bell that had been dealt a hammer blow.

"What was that?" shouted Rosalind.

Ron swung his attention back to the instruments, but he didn't get the chance to answer. There was the thud of an explosion and he was violently thrown against the straps of his pilot's harness.

"We're going for a ride!" Ron yelled back. "Hang on!"

The module tumbled through space as Ron struggled to focus his eyes on the displays. A video screen showed the supply craft breaking away from Blue 6, scattering debris as it went. The starry sky whirled in all directions and Space City itself disappeared from the portholes.

He took a deep breath, then seized the joystick. The first step was to regain control of the module. For a moment, he thought that sometimes, not too often, life in space could be just a bit more boring.

Pretend it's a training exercise, he told himself. He nudged the joystick as delicately as possible, hitting the ignition button with quick taps. The module shuddered every time the attitude rockets turned on, gradually counteracting its wild motion.

It seemed to take forever for the module to stop cartwheeling through space. Half the lights on the control panel were blinking red and the various gauges were flashing numbers so fast that the digits blurred together. A video screen displayed the gutted remains of the main thruster, and Ron grumbled in disbelief. "Tycho's nose! What happened there?"

When he finally stabilized the module, the attitude jets had burned most of the remaining fuel. But the stars had stopped dancing in the sky and the Pacific shone a steady blue in the nearest porthole. He let out a ragged sigh of relief and wiped the sweat from his face.

"One of the fuel tanks blew when we were hit," he called out to Rosalind.

"A meteoroid, right?"

She sounded calmer than he was. His hands were trembling, and he felt like screaming.

"I suppose so," he replied as coolly as he could. "It's a bit early, but it could have been a pebble from the Perseid meteor stream. Either that, or a bit of space debris that was not in the sims."

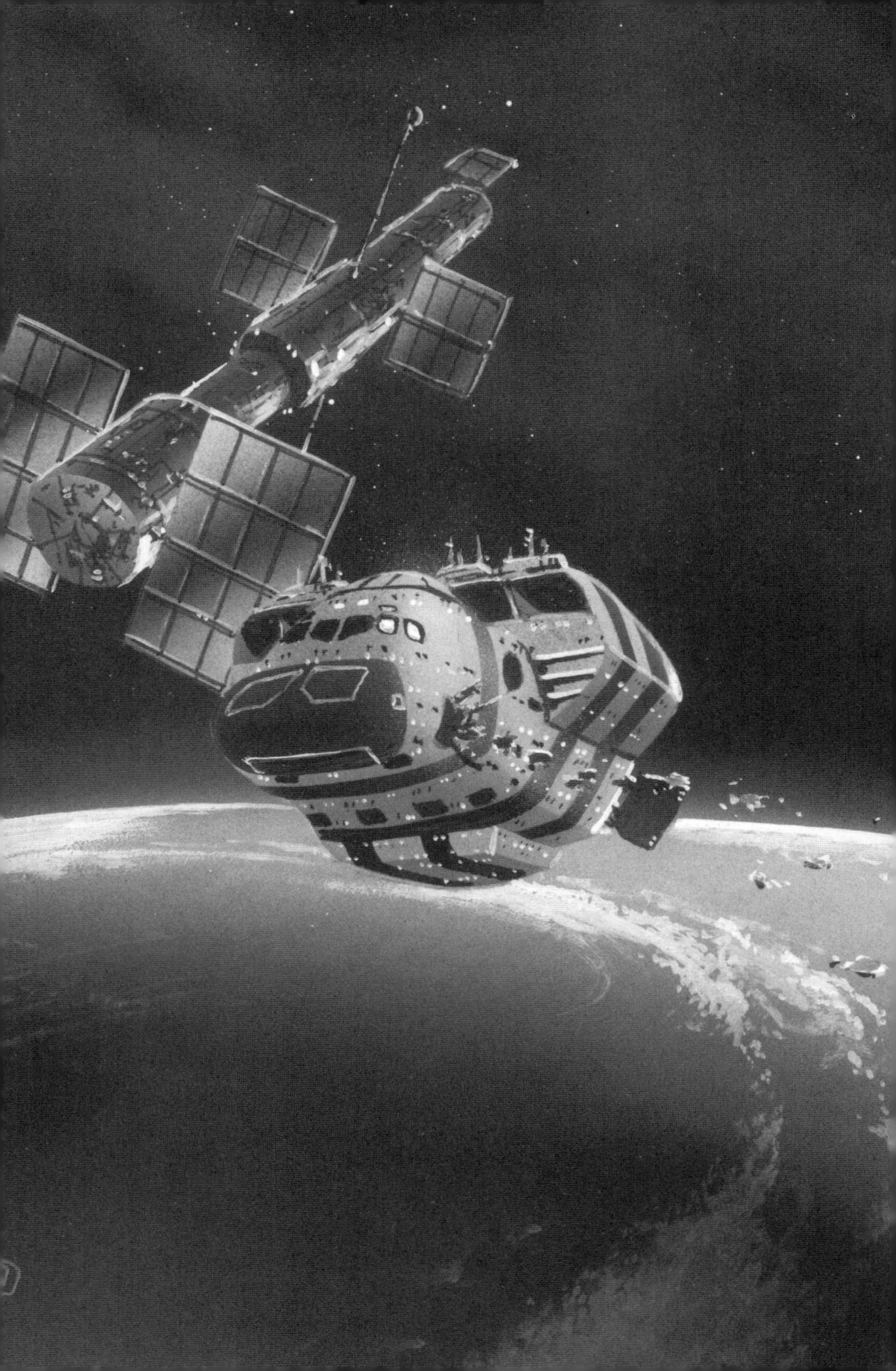

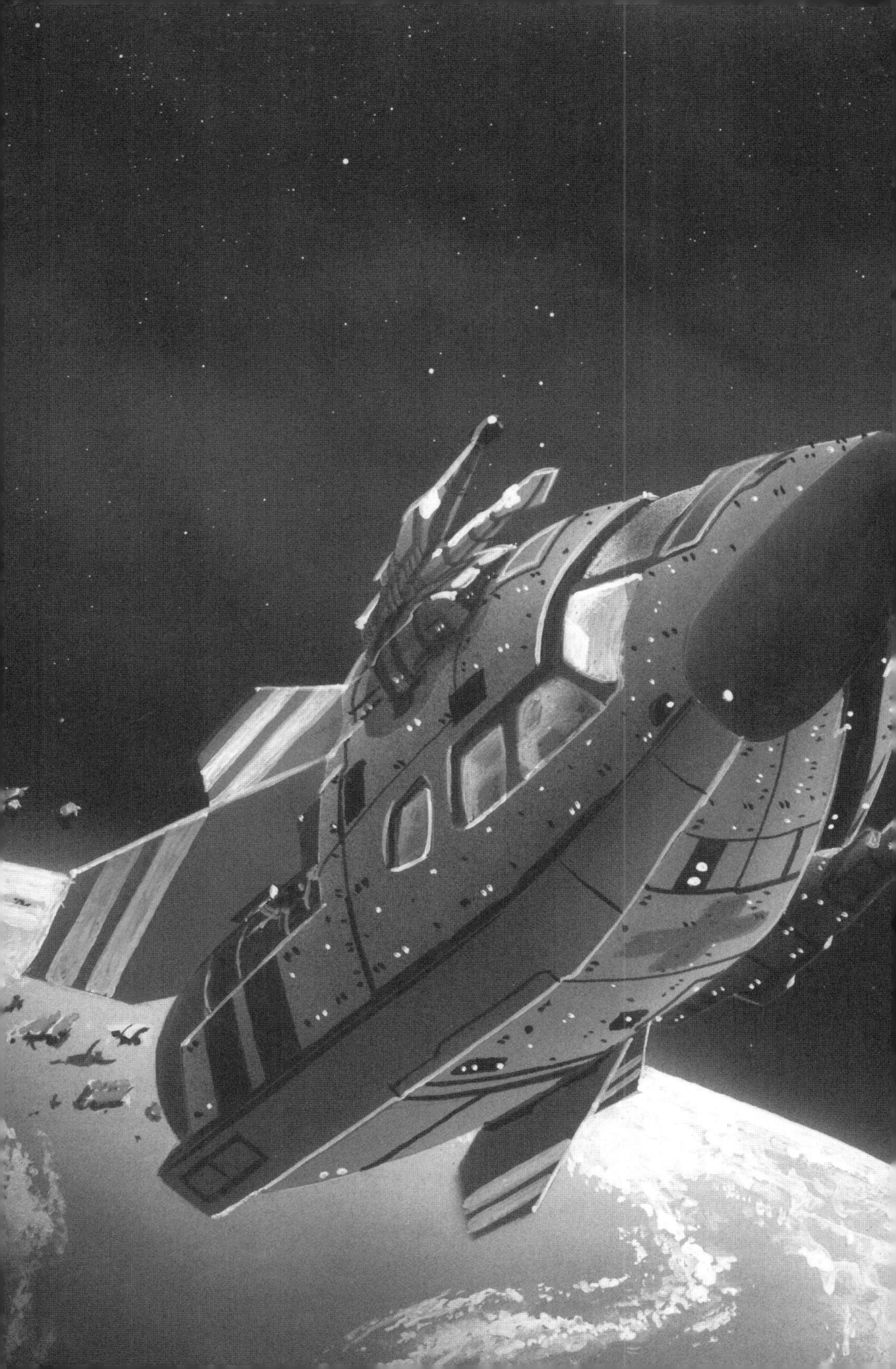

"But the radar didn't pick it up!"

"Well, the supply craft we docked with was blocking part of the sky. Sheer bad luck that something came out of that blind spot so fast the radar didn't have time to alert us. But I'm not worried about that, Roz. The main problem is that it knocked out our propulsion unit. We're adrift."

"Well, can we call someone?"

Impatience had crept into her voice. Ron nodded. She was starting to feel the strain, and it showed. The Earth-born never understood what the orbital work bonus was for until they'd felt it in their bones.

It was an unsettling realization. Though they were a mere few hundred kilometers above the surface of the Earth, they were surrounded by nothingness. Beyond the thin metal shell of the module, there was nothing that could help them survive. Almost any place on Earth, even the top of Mount Everest, even the South Pole in the dead of winter, was less hostile. They were utterly dependent on the fragile resources of their little island, unless they could summon help... Except that they were supposed to answer calls for help, not make them.

He checked the main board again. The electricity gauge showed a steady drop in output voltage.

"Uh oh... The power cell's going. The explosion must have damaged it."

He clearly heard Rosalind's sudden gulp.

"The guy back here needs power," she said quietly, very quietly.

"Don't worry," he said, "we've got options."

"There's a battery, isn't there?"

He twisted his head to inspect the back of the module. His partner had done well. She'd managed to keep the man they'd rescued strapped down through the roughest part of the ride. He was still breathing, just barely, kept alive by the life-support unit.

"Exactly," Ron answered. "And you're going to need most of its power for the life support. I'll start shutting off the lights."

The lights had already started to dim, as the fuel cell slowly failed. Ron switched to the emergency lighting, turned off the heat, turned off the radar, and finally turned off the ventilation. The sudden silence was eerie.

"How long will the battery last?" she asked.

When he turned his head, he could no longer see the expression on her face, lost in the reddish half-light.

"Not long enough ... for three of us."

Ron wondered what the stranger's name was. Somehow, the fact that he didn't know their charge's name would make it worse if the man died. He spoke again in the silence. "But don't worry, Roz, we still have options."

The module was equipped with small solar panels, built into the hull in case of emergencies. Ron made sure Blue 6 was properly orientated, with the panels facing the sun, and then closed the circuit.

The power gauge showed a surge, but it was unexpectedly small. Ron's eyes widened. The panels were producing only a trickle of the power they should have fed to the module.

Rosalind, unable to see the board, called out. "Well?"

Ron thought in a hurry. "When the fuel tank blew, it must have fouled the solar panels with some sort of gunk... The sunlight is just not getting through."

He waited a few more minutes, to be sure. Whether a connection had been loosened by the rough ride earlier or whether the panels were spattered with soot from the explosion, no power was getting through. A yellow warning light started blinking to let him know that all on-board electronics would shut down in less than an hour.

Some of the idle screens turned off to save power.

"We still have one option," Ron muttered.

He had to bend and look beneath the pilot's couch to find the casing, covered with a black and yellow checker-board pattern. When he pulled the lever, the wire started to unspool into space with a clunk and a whir.

"What is that?" asked Rosalind upon hearing the mechanical noise.

"Our lifeline, Roz. Our last chance to keep Blue 6 powered up."

"What do you mean?"

"Don't you know?"

"I'm a medic, Ron, not a space mechanic!" she snapped.

Earth girls don't know anything! But Ron no longer believed that. He sighed and prepared an explanation, since there was nothing else to do. The tether was three kilometers long and it would take nearly half an hour to reach its full extension.

"A century ago, jumbo jets were equipped with a small propeller-driven emergency generator. If absolutely everything failed, the plane's motion through the air would produce the electricity needed. Well, we've got something similar…"

He described the tether: a third of the wire was a bare conductor, while the rest of its length was sheathed with an insulator. Each end of the wire was equipped with a hollow cathode.

"It may not feel like we're moving, but we're actually falling right through your home planet's magnetic field. The wire is therefore moving through that field. Because the wire is a conductor, it has free electrons. So, a force is exerted on the electrons by the magnetic field and they flow in one direction toward the far end of the conductor."

"Induction!" shouted Roz.

"Exactly."

"Wait a minute, Ron, just how do we get a current? The electrons move toward one end of the wire… Okay, I can see that. But what happens next? For us to draw power, they would have to move in a loop… How do you get a circuit out of this?"

"The circuit is right there, even though we can't see it. It's simple, Roz — we're going to get our power from *nowhere.*"

"You mean, from a vacuum?"

"Ah, but space is not that empty. This close to Earth, the magnetic field traps a charged plasma. That means it's full of ions and electrons, although it's so dilute a cubic kilometre of it wouldn't let you knock down a feather. One end of the wire spits out electrons and the other end collects them, completing the circuit."

"Yeah, but is this going to work, Ron?"

He watched the gauges and dials, going dark one-by-one.

"As far as I know, it's never been tried under emergency conditions," he admitted. "But don't worry, they'll notice we're missing sooner or later."

"I hired on to be a rescuer, not a rescuee," she protested.

"That's the spirit!"

It got darker.

When it happened, Ron almost didn't notice the warning light turning off by itself. He was tired and he'd started to shiver in the increasing cold.

Part of his mind noted the event without reacting. It was only when the instruments turned themselves on one after the other that he realized the power was back on. The radar pinged reassuringly, the radio cycled through frequencies, and the computer screens updated the space debris simulations. The ventilation shuddered and the air was suddenly less stale. Finally, the fluorescents turned on and Ron no longer had to fight against the impression that the walls were closing in.

As if he wanted to share in the general awakening, the man from the supply craft struggled back to consciousness a few seconds later. When he opened his eyes, he focused on Rosalind and then shook his head in disbelief.

"Are you kids for real?" he croaked, his voice like a disused robot's.

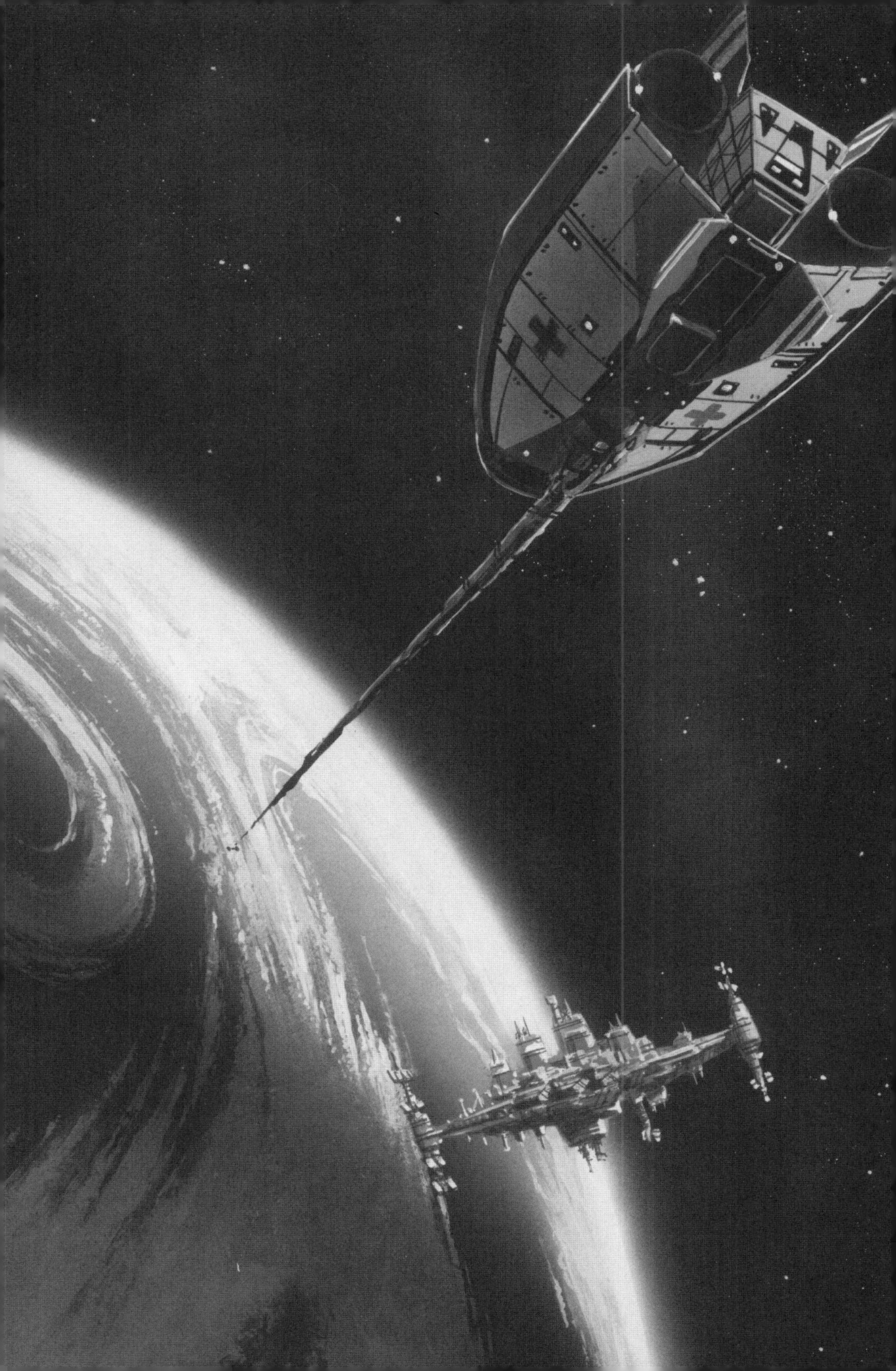

"What's wrong?"

"I thought you'd be older."

"Hey, shuttle jockey, haven't you been paying attention?" Roz replied. "This is the twenty-first century — space is for everybody now. Sure, back in the twentieth, you had to be really old — like 30 or 40 — to get into orbit but that was because you had to be a fighter pilot, speak three languages, and have university degrees coming out your ears before they'd let you go up…"

Ron smiled. *That* was telling him!

The man threw up his arms.

"Okay, okay, I'm sorry. When do we get to Space City?"

Rosalind laughed, and Ron smiled as he turned back to the radio, sending out the call for a voice communication. The stranger didn't realize that his life had been hanging by a thread… But his reaction was exactly what they needed to break the tension. Complaints were wonderfully normal.

Ron decided he could live with a bit of regular old dullness for a while.

When Roz propelled herself past him to reach a porthole, he joined her to look at the view. Who could ever tire of looking at Earth? The planet's landscape changed with every orbit, shaped by seasons and shifting shadows.

"So, Roz, will you come back?"

"Hey, I've got experience now that can't be beat!" She laughed. "And you *know* I can't pass up that orbital work bonus."

She looked out the window at the planet surface above them. White clouds were tearing themselves on the peaks of Japan. "And it's so beautiful too. I think I'd come back even if I wasn't paid extra."

"Don't tell that to our boss…"

The radio crackled behind them.

"I heard that!" intoned the deep voice of their supervisor. "But I'm glad to know you're all right. A few minutes ago, I was looking at the lidar recordings of that incredibly unlucky meteoroid hit and wondering if… We'll send out Blue 5 right away."

The module's orbit had carried them within sight of the vast expanses of Siberia. Ron watched Rosalind's eyes light up as she examined the dark green mantle of forests, bisected by the silvery threads of thawing rivers. For a moment, he envied her.

"It's a beautiful planet," he whispered, "but I'll never go down there."

The bones of the Moon-born were too fragile to face the stresses of Earth gravity. Though none of the Moon-born would ever admit it, their resentment of dirtsiders like Rosalind owed something to their exile from the home planet. And yet it wasn't the fault of the Earth-born.

He started to push away, but Roz caught him by the wrist before he returned to his pilot's couch.

"In that case, Oberon, you leave me no choice," she said, grinning. "I guess I'll have to come to Luna and see the dust races in the Sea of Storms for myself."

"You know, Roz, I'd like that. I really would."

A Strand in the Web

by Anne Bishop

"Oh, yuckit," Zerx said as she looked at the cup in her hand and made squinchy faces. "I asked for it hot, and this is barely even warm!"

"That sounds like the date I had last night," Benj said, snickering as he walked over to his console to begin the morning's work.

No one responded to Benj's remark. That was how we handled these typical morning comments — with polite silence.

77

"I don't see why the maintenance engineers can't fix this thing," Thanie complained, taking her mug from the food slot. She sniffed it to make sure it held tea, then took a cautious sip.

"I heard Marv finally fixed the warning light problem," Whit said as the data for his part of the project filled the screen in front of his console.

"What warning light problem?" Stev asked.

Whit swiveled his chair to face the rest of us. "A warning light on one of the main panels has been flashing intermittently for the past several weeks, warning of a circuit failure in one of the minor systems."

"Probably our food slot," Thanie grumbled.

"Of course, the engineers checked the system out every time and didn't find anything wrong," Whit continued. "When the warning light started flashing again yesterday, Marv gave the control panel a thump with his fist. The warning light went out and hasn't come back on since. Problem solved."

The computer chimed quietly, the signal that the morning class had begun.

As the rest of the team settled into their places, Zerx complained loudly, "Why do *I* have to do the insects?"

Before any of us could remind Zerx — again — that the computer had done a random draw to give us our parts of the assignment and that every part was equally important, Benj said, "Because you *look* like a bug."

Unfortunately, that was true. Zerx had gathered two segments of hair at the front of her head and used some kind of stiffener on them so that they stood straight up and looked quite a bit like insect antennae.

Benj turned away, satisfied with his retort. He didn't see the look on Zerx's face before she went to her own console. Zerx could be very unpleasant when she was in a snit, and that look on her face always meant payback.

Tuning out the usual morning grumbles, I carefully checked my own data, feeling the shiver of excitement go through me as it had for the past month when I sat at this console.

My teammates kept acting like this was another computer simulation that was part of our classwork. Oh, it was part of our classwork all right. In fact, this *was* our classwork now. Only this. But this wasn't a computer simulation where time was accelerated and a planet year was contained within a classroom day. This was *real*.

There were six teams at this stage of our education. We'd had to take an extra year of schoolwork while we waited for our city-ship to reach this world. And *another* extra year after that while we waited for the Restorers to prepare this world for the life we would give back to it.

You couldn't apply for a Restorer's team until you proved you could work in real time and maintain Balance of your part of the project. So we had waited and studied and done the computer simulations and watched our simulated worlds crumble into ecological disaster — much like the worlds the Restorers committed themselves to restoring.

Now each team had part of a large island. Each part had a strong force field around it to prevent any accidents or disasters from going beyond the team's designated area. Now we were working in real time, and we couldn't just delete plants and animals to make it more convenient when something got out of hand. How many of each species we could deposit at our site was limited by our allotment from the huge, honeycombed chambers holding the genetic material for billions of species from all over the galaxy. Now, every life counted — not just for our own final scores in the project, but for the well-being of the planet.

I was assigned the trees for this project, which pleased me very much because my name is Willow.

As I scanned my data, I took a deep breath and let out a sigh of satisfaction. The number of trees had increased since I last checked. I had planted some mature trees, but most of my allotment for this area had been used for saplings and seeds, and the seeds were beginning to grow.

I keyed in the coordinates and the command for a planetside picture on half my screen. A moment later, I was staring at a tiny twig with two leaves — a baby oak tree. Someday its roots would spread deep into the land, its thick trunk would support the strong branches that would provide nesting areas and shelter for birds, its acorns would feed chipmunks and squirrels, and it would produce oxygen that the animals needed to breathe.

A tree was a wonderful piece of creation.

"You look pleased," Stev said as he approached my console.

"Tree," I said, grinning like a fool.

"That *is* your assignment, Willow," he replied, trying to maintain a somber expression. Then he glanced at the screen and his eyes narrowed. He looked at my twig of a tree and then at the numbers for each species. "How'd you get that many trees out of the generation tanks so fast?"

I stiffened a little. But there was nothing in his voice — like there would have been in Benj's or Zerx's — that implied I was getting preferential treatment because both of my parents were Restorers. "I requested 20% of the stock as mature trees old enough to begin self-reproduction, 30% as saplings, and the rest as seeds."

It could take days for the generation tanks to produce a mature specimen, depending on how fast the growing process was accelerated. But it didn't take the tanks more than a few hours to produce healthy, viable seeds.

Stev whistled softly. He didn't say anything for a minute. Then, with his eyes fixed on the little oak tree still on my screen, he said, "The Blessed All has given you a gift for this kind of work, Willow. You'll be on a Restorer's team the moment you're fully qualified."

With a smile that was a little sad, he went back to his own console. And I went back to staring at the little oak.

Restorers. That's what the 87 people who are the heart of our city-ship are called. They give purpose to what would otherwise be an aimless wandering through the galaxy.

The Scholars say that a very long time ago we lived four score and seven years. Our people now live *forty* score and seventy years — 870 years. They say that the Blessed All granted us the knowledge to extend our life spans so that we could make Atonement. That is why the city-ships that are now the home of our people were created — so that we could make Atonement by restoring worlds ravaged either by external disasters or by disasters caused by their inhabitants.

And it is part of our Atonement that we live in a world made of metal, that we never walk on a world we have restored, never feel the breeze that ruffles the leaves, smell the wildflowers ... or press our hands against the bark of a tree that we planted.

The Scholars never say why we have to make Atonement, but they know. You can see the sorrow that's always in their eyes after they complete their training and are told the Scholars' Secrets.

So this restoration of damaged worlds is our way of making Atonement to the Blessed All for some failure long in our past. The Restorers and their teams are the ones who shoulder that responsibility.

I can't remember a time when I didn't want to be a Restorer — not because of the prestige that goes with the title, but because I love to watch things grow.

My console chirped a query, reminding me that I had work to do.

Blanking my screen, I called up the dot map that would show me the placement of the trees. I still had acorns, some sapling ash and birch, and one young

willow left from my first allotment of trees, and I wanted
to use them for the start of a new woodland.

As I brushed my finger over the direction pad on my
console, intending to shift the dot map and look at the
coastline, my hand jerked. I shook it, wondering why it
had done that since the muscles didn't feel cramped.

The Scholars say that sometimes the Blessed All shows
us our path in very small ways.

When I looked at the screen, my hand poised above
the direction pad to shift position back to my team's
designated area, I saw the other island. It was to the
west of the student's island and about one-third the size
— which didn't make it a small island by any means.

Curious about who the Restorer was, I keyed in the
coordinates and asked the question. Every Restorer had a
specific code so that other Restorers could quickly find out
who was working on a particular section of the planet.

There was no Restorer code for that island.

Thinking I'd made a mistake when I keyed in the
coordinates, I tried it again.

No Restorer code.

That wasn't right.

I requested soil analysis data. Maybe the Restorer
teams had missed this island when they had carefully
laid down the microbes and bacteria that were the first
step in restoration. Maybe the land was still too toxic to
support life, and that's why no one was working it.

No, the land was fertile and waiting.

I closed my eyes. It was rash. It was foolish. I would
never be granted a land mass that size for a special

project. And even if I was, I wouldn't be able to achieve Balance without a team to help me.

But I could feel an ache in my bones that I knew was the land's cry to be filled with living things again.

I wanted to answer that cry so much.

A soft warning beep reminded me that I had other land to tend.

I called up the screen that listed the trees and the numbers of each species.

My mouth fell open. For a moment, I couldn't breathe.

During the time when my thoughts had been else-where, 10% of my trees had been destroyed!

Yesterday, Dermi had placed three deer in the meadow that bordered the woodland, which was fine because the meadow was already well established and could feed them.

Now, *fifty* deer had been plunked in the middle of the woodland. There was nothing else for them to eat, so they were devouring my seedling trees.

My fingers raced across the keyboard as I wrote an Urgent request to Dermi for the immediate transfer of the deer to other viable positions within our designated area.

I could have just shouted across the room — and, sometimes, we did that — but every request had to be backed up with written data. The computer could override any request that *wasn't* formally made because, in part, that trail of requests and memos was what our Instructors used to judge our work. And that was sometimes very frustrating. We weren't graded just on our *individual* work, but on the *team's* ability to maintain Balance.

I sat back, trying not to bite my nails while I waited for Dermi's response. It wouldn't take long. Urgents always got top priority.

Minutes passed.

I swiveled my chair and looked at Dermi. She was sitting there, inputting data as calmly as you please.

I sent another Urgent request...and waited.

I attached a verification requirement to the third request to confirm that she *was* receiving the Urgents.

The verification came back. Dermi had gotten the requests and *still* wasn't doing anything.

Throughout the first part of that morning, I continued sending requests while I watched the number of my remaining trees fall ... and fall ... and fall.

When midmorning came, I sent an Urgent request to Fallah, who was handling large carnivores, and asked for a sufficient number of predators who ate deer to be brought to the woodland. At that point, I didn't really care what kind of carnivore she used as long as they would start eating the deer before the deer ate the entire woodland down to the ground.

By the time the computer chimed the signal for the midday break, there were 125 deer in a woodland that wasn't ready to support even one and still maintain Balance.

Instead of transferring deer *out*, Dermi had responded to each Urgent request by sending more deer *in*.

And Fallah hadn't sent one carnivore.

I blanked my screen before going to the food court where the older students gathered for the midday meal.

When Stev asked me what was wrong, I brushed him off. I didn't mean to be rude; I just couldn't talk to anyone. Still, he brought his plate over and sat at the same table. Not next to me or anything, but he was there, along with Thanie and Whit.

I picked at my food, choking down only enough to give my body fuel for the rest of the day.

As we headed back to our classroom, Thanie tugged on my tunic sleeve to slow me down. Not that I was eager to go back in and find out how much damage had been done in the past hour.

"I overheard Dermi and Fallah talking," Thanie said in a low voice. "You're not going to get any carnivores."

"Why not?" I said loudly enough to have Thanie shushing me.

"Because Dermi's in a snit because Stev went to the concert with you last night, and Fallah is Dermi's best friend."

"Stev didn't go to the concert with *me*," I hissed back at her. "A group of us went together — including you."

"*I* know that. But Dermi wanted Stev to ask *her*. So *she's* not going to give you any help and neither is Fallah."

I'd spent a month creating that woodland. A month's worth of work, and all that *life* I had drawn from the genetic material so carefully stored…. All of it wasted because Dermi was jealous.

As I walked to my console, I looked at Dermi. She and Fallah had their heads together, whispering. There was something smug and mean about the way they stared at me.

I called up the data on my screen, and for the rest of the afternoon, I watched my woodland die.

I didn't give Dermi and Fallah the satisfaction of seeing me cry.

I also didn't plant any trees to replace the ones that had been devoured.

I just sat there ... and watched.

Toward the end of the day, when we were supposed to write the day's activity report for our Instructors to review, Zerx sprang her nasty little surprise — her payback for Benj's bug remark.

I wasn't paying attention to much of anything until Whit yelled, "ZERX!" He sent a planetside view to each of our consoles.

Swarm after swarm of locusts were descending like black clouds onto the meadowlands. Zerx must have used almost her entire allotment of insect life to create them.

And there was nothing any of us could do until class began again the next morning.

I think that's why I did it.

Instead of writing my activity report, I used my personal computer pad to write a request for a special project, a piece of land where I would have complete control, where I would be the only one responsible for achieving — and maintaining — Balance.

I asked for the other island.

I requested a Restorer screen around it, which meant that life-forms could be transferred through the force field around the island with my consent, but nothing could slip through on its own. I requested monitor blanking — a

Restorer could override that request, but no one else would be able to see what I was doing unless he or she knew my password.

I sent in my request, blanked my console screen, and went to the living quarters I shared with my parents.

Mother always says that a person must have a life beyond the work. She belongs to a musical society. Father belongs to a theater group. They seldom "talk shop" at dinnertime unless something special happened. Or they talk about their work as a way to answer the questions that usually spill out of me while I tell them about my classwork.

I didn't talk about what happened in class that day. Since they both seemed concerned about something that I sensed they wouldn't talk about while I was there, I also didn't tell them about requesting a special project. After all, I wasn't sure I would get it anyway. Student special projects were usually limited to a few acres of land, not a whole island.

As soon as dinner was finished, I mumbled something about needing to prep for class tomorrow and went to my room. Normally, I would have spent at least an hour going over details and getting requests ready to submit to the techs who oversaw the generation tanks.

Instead I took the hologram from its special place on the shelf, set it on my workspace, and turned it on.

When I was a little girl, my mother asked me what I wanted for my birthday, which was still a couple of weeks away. I told her I wanted a tree.

The day of my birthday, just before the time when Mother usually programmed the food slot for the evening meal, Father muttered something about having a bit of business to take care of and left.

Before I could express my disappointment that he wasn't going to celebrate my birthday with us, Mother held out her hand and smiled. "We have a bit of business to take care of, too."

We went to the room where her team worked. It was the end of the day shift, and there were only a couple of her assistants in the room. When they saw us, they smiled and left. At the time, I was too young to realize that a Restorer's room was *never* left unattended and there was something unusual about them *all* leaving like that.

Mother led me to the large console where she worked. She sat me on her lap, and with her hand over mine, she opened a screen that showed a planetside picture of a creek. Her hand guided mine as we set the coordinates and issued the command codes.

A few minutes later, a young willow tree stood near the bank of the creek.

"There's your tree, Willow," Mother said quietly.

I don't know how long we sat there, Mother with her arms around me and her cheek resting against my head, just watching the light breeze flutter the willow's leaves.

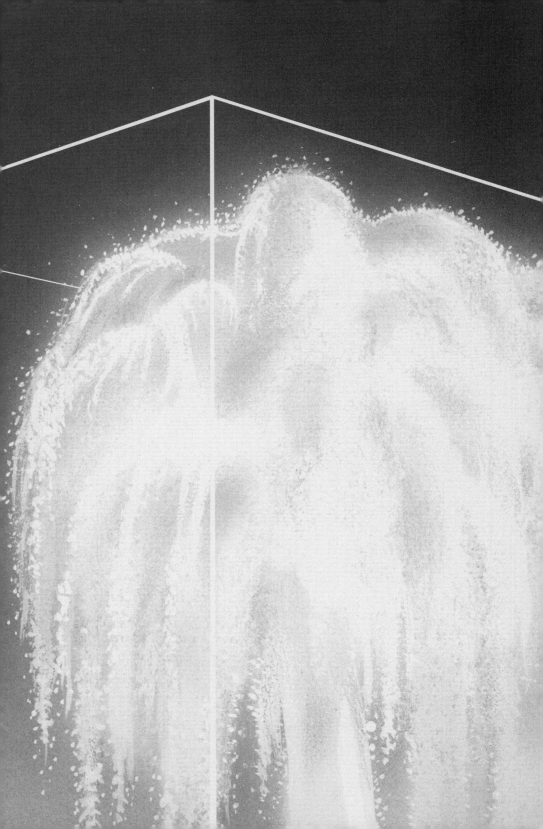

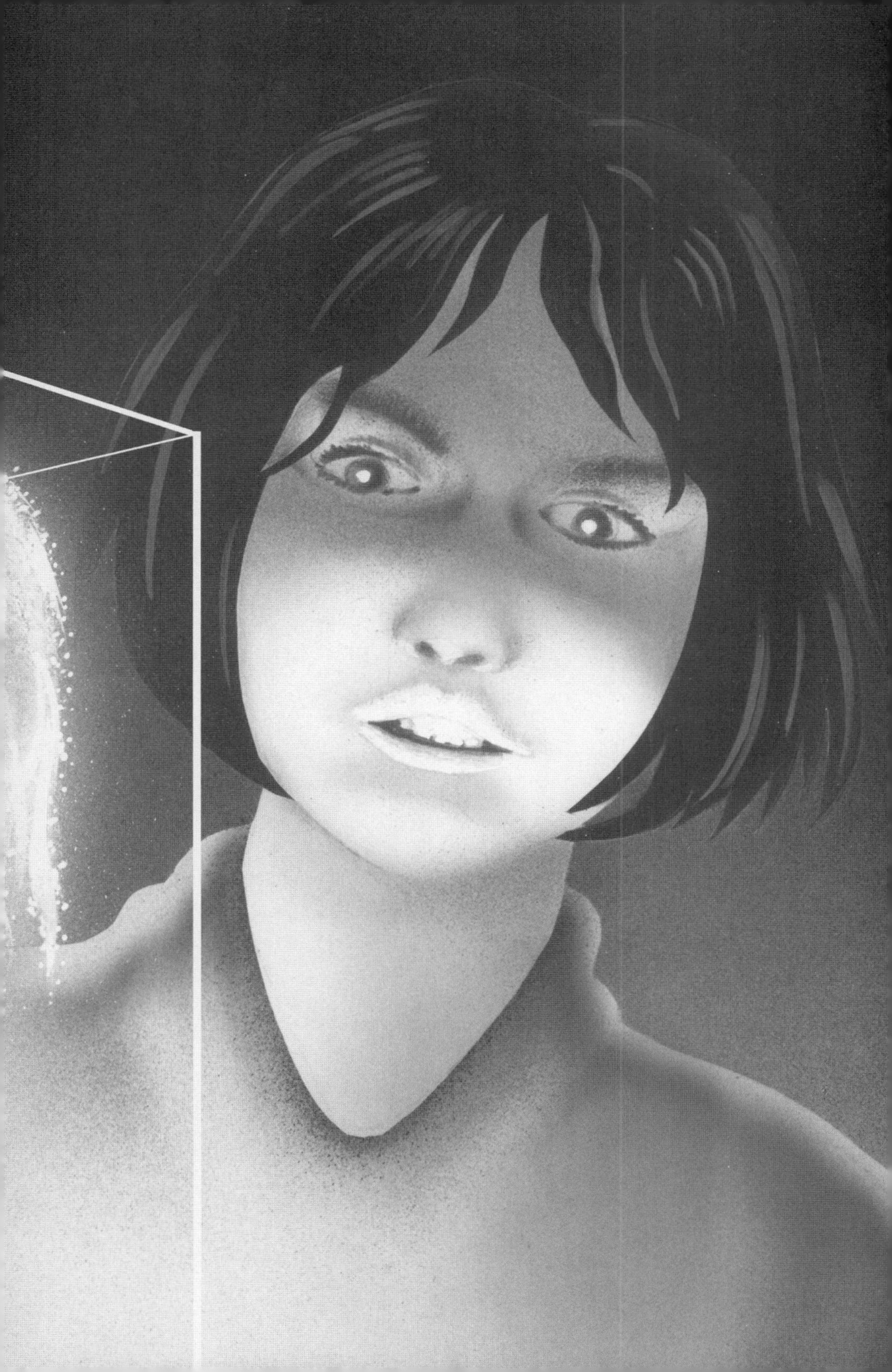

When she finally blanked the screen and we returned to our living quarters, Father was waiting for us, his smile a little hesitant.

And I knew then that, just as my mother had arranged for me to plant that tree, my father had personally overseen its growth in the generation tanks. But that wasn't his business that evening.

After dinner and the birthday sweet, I was given my other present — a hologram of that young willow by the creek. While Mother and I had been planting the tree, Father had arranged to have the hologram made so that I would be able to keep that moment.

In all the years that have come and gone since then, that hologram has remained my most treasured gift.

I turned off the hologram and carefully put it back on the shelf.

There was nothing I wanted to do about the class project. There was nothing I *could* do about the special project. So I read for a while and then went to bed.

And spent a restless night full of terrible dreams about destruction.

2

I checked my personal computer pad the moment I woke up. I checked it before I left for class. I checked it the moment I got to the classroom.

Nothing. No confirmation or denial for my special project.

The locusts had been busy since class ended yesterday, and everyone could see this was leading to disaster. Requests zipped back and forth, mostly requests to the Instructor who was our advisor to be allowed to terminate the locusts down to a workable population. The same message came back every single time: termination was unacceptable. Balance had to be restored by natural means — which meant transferring into that area or producing enough birds, reptiles, and mammals to consume the locusts.

Requests poured to Stev's and Whit's consoles since they were the team members who were trying to qualify for Right Hand status — that is, becoming a Restorer's primary technical assistant — and had some "pull" with the generation tank techs. They forwarded the requests, which were acknowledged and put in the queue of student requests. That meant all we had to work with was what we already had.

That caused a lot of muttering and grumbling.

The locusts weren't the only problem. The deer had eaten my young woodland right down to the ground. All I really had left to work with were the mature trees and the acorns and saplings I still hadn't planted. And I had no intention of sacrificing *them.*

Then Benj thought to check the team rating and discovered that it had dropped so low *none* of us would qualify for *any* kind of starting position on a Restorer's team.

That's when the yelling *really* started.

Of course, Zerx, Dermi, and Fallah were the ones who yelled the loudest.

The rest of the morning was filled with scrambled panic. Dermi started transferring the deer any old place within our designated area. Fallah finally released some of her carnivores and plunked them down in the middle of the deer. Benj dumped mice, squirrels, and rabbits into meadowlands already covered with locusts, not giving any thought to whether or not any of those animals would help with the locust problem. Thanie transferred her songbirds to that area, and Dayl poured in a load of reptiles.

It was a mess.

I did very little throughout the morning. I politely answered requests for more trees and made no promises. When the requests became more forceful, I said my order for saplings was already in the student queue and I would begin establishing the woodland as soon as trees were available.

It was almost time for the midday break when I keyed in the coordinates for the other island.

I stared at the screen for a long minute, my heart, and my hopes, sinking.

The island now had a Restorer code.

The midday meal was ... unpleasant. Stev, Thanie, Whit, and I sat at a table by ourselves. None of us wanted to talk. Thanie was the only one who tried — once.

"It's early in the project," she said, looking hopefully at each of us. "We'll be able to restore Balance soon and get our rating back."

"The only good thing about all of this is that the force field won't allow our stupidity to spill into anyone else's area," Stev replied with enough bitterness that none of us dared say anything else.

Judging from the angry looks that were flashing between other tables around the food court, our team wasn't the only one having problems. Which didn't make me feel any better.

It was toward the end of the class day when I finally checked my personal computer pad again. My parents sometimes left messages to let me know if they would be working late or if there was a particular chore I should take care of.

There *was* a message for me. I read it three times before I finally understood what it said.

My request for the island had been granted. The code I had seen was the one that had been assigned to *me* for the duration of the project.

Feeling dizzy, I hugged the computer pad and tried to draw in enough air to breathe properly.

A warm hand settled on my shoulder.

"Willow?" Stev said, sounding concerned. "Are you all right?"

"I'm fine," I said, trying not to gasp out the words.

Stev studied me carefully. "You don't look fine."

"No, I'm fine. Really." I started shutting down my console any old way.

Stev brushed my hand aside and closed the console in the proper sequence.

"Come on," he said. "I'll walk you home."

"I'm fine," I said again. At that moment, I wasn't sure if I was going to dance down the corridors or burst into tears. I *did* know that I really needed to be alone for a while to think this through.

Stev walked me to my family's living quarters. He didn't ask any of the questions I could see in his eyes, and I was grateful.

I spent an hour in my room staring at that message.

The island was mine. *Mine.*

I couldn't possibly build a viable ecosystem for a land mass that size and maintain Balance all by myself. In fact, it would be totally foolish to even *try* to establish an ecosystem over the whole island all at once.

I wasn't sure how much time I would have. Sooner or later, someone would realize that a student had been given an island that should have been handled by a primary Restorer. But if I could establish a full ecosystem in a few thousand acres to *prove* I could do it, maybe I would be allowed to continue — or at least to be part of the team that finished restoring the island.

I couldn't do it alone. Life-forms, from the smallest to the largest, had to be established. Each link in the chain of survival had to be formed carefully and in the right order. I needed someone who would act as a Restorer's Right Hand, who would support my work without trying to change it to suit his own vision, who could work independently, someone who could be counted on to value Balance.

I needed Stev.

Since I had an hour before my parents got home, I keyed in the island's coordinates and requested lists of all the species that were viable for this world and for that particular island.

The computer immediately requested the password.

Huh? I hadn't *set* a password yet.

I went back to the message that had given me the Restorer code. At the bottom of the message was the password: unicorn.

An odd word, I thought as I sounded it out. And it seemed equally odd that the password had been chosen for me. But this was no time to quibble. I made my request for species lists, added the password, and waited.

The lists were daunting. I'd had no idea that so many of the species that were stored in those vast honeycomb chambers were suitable for this world. No wonder the Restorers were looking a little dazed.

The computer chimed the warning that the hour was up. I saved the lists under my password, closed down the computer, and went to make dinner since it was my turn.

When I pressed the pad next to the food slot to indicate I was about to place my order, I was still muttering, "Earthworms, grubs, tadpoles, flies." Fortunately, the computer suggested that I place another order from the available menu. I could just imagine Father's reaction if I set a platter of tadpoles and bugs over earthworm pasta in front of him. No, this wouldn't be a good time for a lecture on keeping my mind focused on the task at hand. Not a good time at all.

I chose meatloaf, which would please Father, and a variety of vegetables to go with it, which would please Mother.

I had the table set when Father came home. Mother arrived a few minutes later, looking distracted.

She filled her plate without any comments, then sat there, pushing her peas around with her fork.

After a few minutes, Father said, "Has Britt made a decision?"

"She's stepping down as a primary Restorer," Mother replied.

"Britt?" I said, snapping to attention. "Why is Britt stepping down? Is she sick again?" Britt was the oldest Restorer on our ship. Forty score and seventy were the years allotted to us for Atonement. Britt had celebrated her 800th birthday several months ago, shortly before she became very ill. She had recovered and seemed fine whenever I saw her, although I remember Zashi, her RRH and life partner, had been very concerned for a while.

"Zashi is also stepping down," Mother said, still rearranging her peas. "He says he wants to concentrate on his tale telling."

Zashi was a wonderful tale teller. Whenever one of his story hours was listed in the activities, I was there. But if Britt and Zashi were no longer going to lead a team…

"What's going to happen to Britt's team?" I asked.

"Oh, they'll help out wherever they're needed for a while," Mother said, sounding vague — which wasn't like Mother at all.

"Then Britt didn't name a successor?" Father asked, frowning at his meatloaf.

"Not yet."

And even if she had, a new Restorer would form a new team, so there would be the inevitable shuffling as people settled into new assignments.

Father sighed. "Looks like some of us will have to shoulder the extra work in order to take care of the area that Britt had intended to restore."

"No," Mother said, a funny catch in her voice. "Someone has taken responsibility for restoring Balance to the island."

I choked.

Mother gave me a light thump on the back. "Better?"

I nodded, not trusting myself to speak.

I'd been given Britt's island. *Britt's.* Blessed All, she was the most talented Restorer to come along in several generations. Everyone said so.

"Are you all right, Willow?" Mother asked, brushing her hand over my forehead. "You look pale."

That got Father's full attention.

"I'm fine," I lied. "Really."

Mother smiled, but it wasn't her usual, easy smile. I could tell she was straining not to say a lot of things. Which made me wonder if she knew who had taken responsibility for restoring Balance to Britt's island.

I spent the evening in my room. Father had gone to a rehearsal for a play that his theater group was doing. Mother was listening to music.

My feelings kept going round and round. First feeling overwhelmed by the task I'd been given, then excited, then scared.

Finally I sat in meditation to become attuned to the Blessed All. In that silence, I found the quiet stillness within me. And then all I felt was joy.

I could do this. I *would* do this. I would bring life back to the island — not only for my sake and the land's sake, but now for Britt as well.

3

The next morning, just before the computer chimed the start of class, I sidled over to Stev's console.

"Stev, I've received permission for a special project. Would you help me?"

His eyes lit up with pleasure. "Sure, Willow." Then he added reluctantly, "Will you credit me for my work?"

I hesitated a moment too long. And remembered a moment too late that other people had asked for Stev's help on a project and *hadn't* given him credit for his work. I'm sure the Instructors were aware of his part of it, and there was probably a private note in his file acknowledging the work, but it wasn't *formally* listed on his credits — and that could make a difference in earning the qualifications necessary to work on a Restorer's team.

His eyes dimmed. His face hardened. "Just tell me what you need," he said — and turned his back on me.

He didn't sit with Thanie, Whit, and me during the mid-day break. He didn't say a thing to me the whole day.

When the computer chimed the end of the class day, I gathered my courage and approached him.

"Could you stay a few minutes?" I asked quietly, noticing the sullen looks Dermi was giving me and the way she was lingering so that she would leave at the same time Stev did.

She left in a huff when Stev finally noticed her and gave her a cold stare.

Dermi was one of the people who hadn't given him credit for his work on one of her projects. Why she kept expecting him to ask her for a date after pulling that stunt was something the rest of us couldn't figure out.

"What is it?" Stev asked, not sounding the least bit friendly.

I took a deep breath. "If this project succeeds, I'll be very happy to give you credit for your work. But if it doesn't — "

"Succeed or fail, I either get credit or I don't," he snapped.

"I think you should see the project before you say that."

I went to my console, keyed in the coordinates, and then asked for a red line to show the boundaries of the project.

When the red line appeared, all I could do was stare. The message granting my request for the special project *had* contained the dimensions of the area that was now my responsibility, but I'd been so stunned and excited about getting the island, I hadn't paid attention to the numbers. It hadn't occurred to me that my designated area would be *larger* than I'd requested.

Not only was I responsible for the island, I was also responsible for a band of salt water that surrounded the island. Which meant that I was responsible for a small part of another, entirely different ecosystem.

Stev studied my screen for a minute. "Have you got that little island off the main one that a Restorer is working on?"

"Not exactly," I said weakly. Stev was looking at a tiny island off the east coast. It probably had been connected to my island at one time.

"So what *is* your project, Willow?" Stev said a bit impatiently.

"Well…" I gestured vaguely at the screen. "Everything inside the red line."

Stev's mouth fell open. "*Willow!*" He braced himself against the back of my chair. "Do you know how *big* that is?"

I certainly did.

Stev took a couple of deep breaths. "So who do you have for your team?"

"Well… Actually… You."

It was more luck than intention that he ended up sitting in my chair and not on the floor.

"Are you *crazy?*" he shouted.

I knelt in front of him, grabbed his hands, and held on tight. "We can do it, Stev. I know we can! And we don't have to do *all* of it all at once. Look." I jumped up, keyed in the boundary lines of the area I'd decided to work on first. "We can start here, with just this much. That's enough land to create Balance. We can work out from there."

I wasn't sure if Stev couldn't think of anything to say or didn't dare say what he was thinking.

"We can do it," I said again.

"That's a Restorer code," he said slowly as he studied the image on the screen.

"That's the code I was given for this project."

He took another deep breath. "With a Restorer code, we wouldn't be stuck in the student queue. We could use any generation tank that was available."

"We'll have to start from the ground up," I said as my brain began its stubborn chant of earthworms, grubs, tadpoles, flies.

"This really is crazy." Then he smiled. "Count me in. Have you made any lists for what's suitable for that land?"

"I'll transfer copies to your personal computer pad," I said happily.

Stev looked at the lists. Then he finally looked at me. "You're the Restorer on this project. Where do you want to start?"

I'd already thought of that. Balance. Always Balance. Every living thing needed a food source. "The simpler life-forms, especially the ones that aerate the soil. Seeds for grasses and wildflowers."

Stev nodded. "I'll do some checking. The generation tanks may already be producing some of these for other teams. With life-forms like this, the techs usually use enough genetic material to create in batches, then portion it out. That way no team is dependent on the genetic variables that might be in a single batch. We decide on a total number that we want in the designated area, then ask that a percentage of the total come from each batch until we reach our allotment. The grass seed won't be a problem. I'll go down to the tank rooms now and get that started. There should be some to distribute by tomorrow afternoon."

I smiled. He was talking to himself more than to me, which is what he usually did when he was focused and interested in the task.

He finally stopped, looked at me, let out a shout of laughter, gave me a fast hug, and headed for the door. When I didn't follow, he stopped. "Aren't you coming?"

Still smiling, I shook my head. "I have to close down. Then I'll work at home. You can reach me on my personal pad."

When he was gone, I keyed in the coordinates that I had searched for last night. My screen filled with a planetside picture of a stream dancing over rocks.

Each link in the chain of survival had to be formed carefully and at the right time. But the simpler life-forms and the grasses would not be the first bit of life I gave back to this land.

There, by the stream, I planted the young willow tree that I had saved from my student allotment.

4

I got to class early the next morning. Stev was already there.

"The first batch of grass seed finished early this morning and is now in a holding tank," he said. "There's also a memo asking that the holding tanks be emptied as quickly as possible since there's a lot of material going down to the planet and full holding tanks will slow up the use of the generation tanks."

"Then let's get to work." I'd spent part of last evening working out where we should start. Accessing the data Stev had sent to my personal pad, we had enough seed to cover several hundred acres. I keyed in coordinates for half the acreage and sent the command to the holding tank for dispersal of half the seed. As the commands were relayed through the city-ship's various systems and dispersal began, a green tint began filling in the dot map that I had called up on my screen. When it was done, I sat back and grinned.

"You've still got the other half of the seeds to plant," Stev pointed out.

"No," I said, "*you've* got the other half to plant."

His eyes widened when I sent the password to his personal pad. His fingers danced through the command codes.

Grinning like fools, we watched the green tint fill in another part of the island.

We both jumped to change the image on our screens when the door slid open and Whit walked in.

"I don't know why the two of you are looking so pleased," he grumbled. "If we can't get this project under control, we'll have to ask for complete termination and start over. And *that* will definitely be on our formal records."

The rest of the team began to file in. Dermi and Fallah walked past me as if I didn't exist. Thanie slunk into the room, looking like she'd had a very bad night. Even Benj didn't make any of his usual comments. And none of the others had anything to say as they took their places and called up the data for their part of the project.

Whit was right. It was awful. So much of the plant life had been consumed that there wasn't enough for the animals in the area to eat. And there was no chance that the remaining plants would reproduce and repopulate the area fast enough. If we dumped the next class allotment of plant life into the area without doing some-thing to adjust the number of animals and insects, it would be consumed immediately.

What it came down to was this: if we were going to restore Balance, we would have to wait out the depletion of life. That, too, was part of Balance. Creatures consumed one kind of life and were, in turn, consumed.

For a while, the predators — both those that walked on the land and those that soared in the sky — would feast. They would mate and produce young who would also feast. But their prey, who ate the plants and seeds, would starve and produce no young. The predators, in their turn, would starve. And the land would start building the links in the chain of survival again — the grasses and flowers, the shrubs and the trees, the insects that would pollinate them, and on and on until, once more, there was Balance.

But sometimes a world goes too far out of Balance. Sometimes too many links in the chain are broken too severely, and a world spirals into destruction.

Those are the worlds we restore to Balance as our Atonement to the Blessed All.

The computer chimed the start of class, and I got to work.

There were several requests from Dermi, of all people, for seedling trees. Checking the coordinates she had indicated, I realized she wanted me to put down seedlings in the middle of the deer herds to give them a food source. My next allotment of trees would only feed the deer for a few days at most, and that wasn't going to help the situation.

But I was still part of the team, and I had to do something to honor the request.

Remembering what Stev had said about the holding tanks, I released all the sapling birch and ash with a Priority attached to the planting command. I planted half the acorns I still had. I ordered the other half for above-ground dispersal. I winced about that, but they *would* provide some food for the nut eaters.

I didn't plant or disperse any of them where the deer concentrations were the highest. I felt bad for the deer, but sustaining them today only to have them starve tomorrow wasn't going to help the team restore Balance to our area.

I also put in a request to Whit's console for oak and beech trees that were mature enough to reproduce. I didn't think it wise to send *all* my requests through Stev, even though I preferred working with his specimens. Whit would use the full acceleration feature of the generation tanks; Stev never did without a very strong reason.

I breathed a sigh of relief when the computer chimed the midday break.

"Well, that was an interesting morn— " Stev started to say as the door slid open and we stepped into the corridor.

It was *cold.*

"Blessed All," Whit said. "Some of the heating system must have gone down." He shivered. "Come on. Let's get to the food court and get some hot food."

"If there *is* any hot food," Thanie grumbled, hurrying after him.

The rest of the team rushed past us. Stev didn't move.

"Stev?" I put my hand on his arm. His muscles were so tight, they didn't feel like flesh anymore. And he was very pale.

"This is how it started the last time," he whispered.

"No, Stev," I said, shaking my head. "*No.* Part of a system went down. The engineers are probably already working on it, and it'll be fixed in no time."

His eyes were haunted when he finally looked at me. "Of course it will," he said.

He didn't believe it. He had reason not to believe it.

But we couldn't afford to believe anything else. As part of our Atonement, we lived in a world made of metal. If something really *was* wrong with the ship, there was nowhere else for us to go. Nowhere.

Dermi returned from the midday break in a major snit. When she checked her data and realized what I'd done, the snit exploded into a prime tantrum.

"You..." she said, stomping across the room toward me. You..." She called me a very rude thing. "You did this deliberately."

"I provided what I had available," I replied, trying to remain calm as I stood up to face her. "I've also requisitioned my next tree allotment."

"That's not going to help my deer *now*, is it?" Dermi shouted.

"Hey, Dermi," Zerx said, looking wary and guilty since it was *her* snit that had given us the locust problem. "Willow is just doing what — "

"Stay out of this, bug-brain," Dermi snarled. "She did it on purpose."

The way you poured deer into a woodland that couldn't support them? "I provided what I had available."

"You're doing this just to make me look bad," Dermi said, so angry she was turning pale. "The deer need food and *you* could have provided it."

I took a deep breath. "You could ask to transfer them. Maybe one of the other student teams need some deer.

One of the Restorer teams might be planning to bring that species of deer into another area. You could — "

"You get *demerits* on your score when you ask to transfer," Dermi shouted. Then her voice dropped to a quiet that was far more menacing. "Of course, *you* never get demerits for *anything.*"

Maybe I should have realized this wasn't really about the deer. Dermi had always wanted the special student privileges I had without doing any of the work I'd done to earn them. She always wanted something from people without ever being willing to give anything in return. Maybe I should have realized how much she resented my friendship with Stev — maybe I would have been prepared for what happened.

But I really didn't expect her to *hit* me because harming someone violated our strictest rules.

And I can't honestly say which of us was more stunned when her hand connected with my face.

I staggered back into the arm of my chair. As the chair swiveled, my body twisted with it. I reached out to grab the console, but I was too off balance to catch myself. My right hand slid. My head hit the console with an awful *thud.*

I must have blacked out for a few seconds. When I could see again, Dermi was sitting in the middle of the room crying her eyes out and Whit was doing his best to hold on to Stev, who had his teeth bared and his fists clenched.

I tried to push myself into a sitting position, but something was wrong with my right wrist. I yelped in pain and flopped back down on the floor.

At least that made Stev think of something besides punching Dermi, which would have gotten him into trouble.

The next thing I knew, I was cradled against Stev's chest and Thanie was kneeling in front of me, crying quietly, holding out a wadded up piece of linen that had a lot of colored threads dangling out of it. After songbirds, Thanie loved embroidery, and she always carried a little sack of stuff with her.

She tried to press the linen against my face. It hurt, so I tried to push her hand away.

"You're *bleeding*," Thanie said.

Well, that explained why my face felt wet.

At least Thanie had remembered to take the linen out of the embroidery frame. I just hoped she'd also remembered to take the needles out of the cloth.

"Can you walk?" Stev asked.

"Sure," I said, not sure of anything at all.

"Close down our consoles for us," Stev said to someone. It must have been Whit since he was the person who answered.

I wanted to go home. Instead, I got walked to sick bay. The medic frowned at the bruise on one side of my face, grumbled about the sprained wrist, and said some very rude things while he took care of the gash on my forehead.

By the time Stev walked me home, my head was pounding so bad that it made me sick to my stomach. I barely made it into the bathroom before I threw up.

That didn't make my head feel any better. But what made me feel worse was realizing Stev was hovering outside the bathroom door, probably wondering which would be more helpful — coming in or staying out.

If he really wanted to be helpful, he would have gone as far away from the bathroom as possible.

Sometimes boys have no understanding at all of how girls think.

Of course, that was what my emotions wanted and not what my body needed. So Stev was right to stay close by and my emotions were wrong for wanting him to go away — which, by the time I left the bathroom, made me very cranky.

Stev told me in a quiet, soothing voice, "the medic said you're going to be fine." "You just need to get some rest now." Stev took my shoes off and tucked me into bed.

Then Father burst into the room.

"The medic contacted your parents," Stev whispered before he stepped away from the bed.

Father had that look on his face — that pale, tight, angry look he got when I was really sick or hurt and there was nothing he could do about it.

He didn't say anything. Not one thing. Not a scold, not a soothe, nothing. He just walked over to the bed and very carefully placed his hand on my head.

"I'm fine," I lied, trying to smile.

Nothing. That was a *very* bad sign. When Father was this angry and wouldn't say *anything*, it meant that he was about to explode.

I wished Mother was there. I didn't think my head could stand Father exploding.

"The medic said someone should stay with her," Stev said quietly. Then he added, "I'll stay, sir."

Father straightened up, turned, and looked at Stev.

Stev straightened up and tensed.

The air between them seemed to crackle.

"I'll check in," Father said. Then he walked out of the room.

Stev let out a deep breath. His fingers lightly brushed my hand. "Get some rest, Willow."

I must have dozed off, because I sort of remember hearing Mother and Stev talking quietly. Then I fell asleep and didn't hear anything at all.

I woke up sometime later.

Stev was sitting in front of my computer, quietly working.

All the muscles that had tensed as I fell were now aching along with my head and wrist. My mouth tasted like what I imagined the bottom of a swamp did, judging by pictures I'd seen of swamps. And I couldn't get my body to listen to my request to sit up.

Stev looked at me, saw me struggling, and hurried over to help me up.

"How are you feeling?" he asked.

How was I feeling? Very aware that I was sitting with a boy who I might like as more than a friend, looking like some swamp dweller and not being well enough to do anything about it. Which Stev wouldn't understand at all, so I said, "Thirsty." I looked at the computer. I just wanted to forget about this afternoon and fuss over my trees for a little while.

114

"You need to stay warm," Stev said as he went over to the storage cupboard that held my clothes. He came back with my robe — the worn-out robe that was my favorite piece of clothing and that I wouldn't ever let anyone but my parents see me wearing.

Before I could tell him to bring something else, I was bundled into the robe.

"Slippers," he muttered, looking around until he spotted them. Those made him pause.

Mother gave them to me last year as a funny present. I don't know where she got the idea for them or how she got them made, but I loved them.

They were fuzzy, blue bunny slippers. I wore them so much the "fur" was all matted. The ears, because I tended to play with them while I was thinking through a class assignment, weren't as stiff as they used to be and would wave at people when I walked.

Stev didn't say a thing as he stuffed my feet into the slippers. He helped me to the other chair at my work-space. "I'll get you some tea," he said, then hurried out of the room.

He brought back mugs of chamomile tea for both of us.

"Your mother has been checking in every hour," he said as he sat down. "Your father has been checking in every fifteen minutes." He sounded both annoyed and approving.

"He's worried about my head," I said.

"Your head isn't what he's worried about."

At least, that's what I *thought* Stev muttered. I let it go. I didn't feel well enough to try to figure out why Father and Stev were acting odd about each other.

"Where are we?" I asked as I tried to focus on the screen. That was a mistake. My head immediately started to pound.

Stev hesitated. "Based on where you had indicated woodlands and meadows, I've made a list of the species that will inhabit those areas."

That was good. At least one of us hadn't wasted the afternoon.

"We'll have to wait until we get back to class tomorrow to plant anything," I said. We could do all the planning on our computers or our personal pads, but we needed a console to send requests to the generation tanks or command codes for the distribution of species on the planet.

Stev put his mug down. He took mine and set it down before taking my hands in his.

"Willow..." He sighed. "You've been dismissed from the class project. The message came in a little while ago."

"Dismissed?" I stared at him in shock. "I've been *expelled* from the Restorer program?"

"No," he said firmly. "It didn't say you were expelled from the program. It said you were dismissed from the class project."

"But that's the same thing," I wailed. "At this stage of training, it's the same thing." Then I really *looked* at him. "They dismissed you, too, didn't they?"

"Yes." He looked down at our linked hands. "When the message came through your computer, I checked my messages and..."

"Was Dermi dismissed?"

"There's no way for me to know that, Willow."

Of course there was — Whit. The team would have to be told that Stev and I were dismissed so that our work could be distributed among the rest of the team. If Dermi had been dismissed as well, Whit would have known by the end of the class day — and he would have told Stev.

So Stev and I were out of the program, and Dermi...

"The island," I gasped. "What about the island?"

"Nothing was said about the island. Your code is still there, the password still works. You still have the island."

"*We* still have the island."

Stev smiled slowly. "We still have the island." He looked at my computer. "But we need to find a console to work from."

"We'll find one. And we'll do the work while we can."

He gave me an odd look. "Yes. We'll do the work while we can." Turning away, he started closing down the computer.

"We can still — "

"Do you want anyone else to know about the island yet?"

"No."

He continued closing down. He must have understood something about my father's check–ins that I didn't, because Father arrived home a few minutes later — well before his usual time.

And there I was, sitting next to Stev with my face bruised and bandaged, wearing my grubby robe and my bunny slippers.

When I saw my father, I flung myself at him and burst into tears. "Daddy, I've been *expelled.*"

I don't know which startled him more — me calling him Daddy, which I hadn't done since I was a little girl, or crying all over him. But he held me and rocked me and told me everything would be all right. And because for that little while he was once again Daddy, I believed him.

By the time I'd wound down to sniffles, Stev was gone and Mother was home.

They didn't fuss over me too much that evening. That was Mother's doing, I think. I stayed in the living area most of the evening, drifting on the music Mother had selected. I could hear them talking very quietly, but I couldn't focus enough to make out any words.

I drifted on the music and found my way to the deep stillness within me — that place where answers are sometimes found if you're willing to listen.

When I finally fell asleep, I knew exactly where to find a console Stev and I could use.

5

It took three days before I felt well enough to work anywhere other than my room. Stev worked from his room, too. It would have been easier if we could have worked in the same place instead of always checking our personal pads for messages. But Stev pointed out that the only way he could have spent the day in my room without Father spending it with us would be to explain the special project.

I could see his point, sort of. Since we didn't have any class work, it would be difficult to explain why we needed to work together without explaining what we were working on.

So I made lists. I planned. When I had finished working my way through the links in the chain of survival for the land, I switched to the freshwater systems: plants, insects, reptiles, fish. By then I was too restless to do nothing more than make lists that I couldn't turn into reality, so I went hunting for a console.

Every Restorer team had a main room where they worked. Each team also had an auxiliary room with a handful of consoles.

I figured that, since Britt and Zashi had stepped down, Britt's team wouldn't be using their auxiliary room. Any assistance they were providing to other teams could be done from their main room.

So that morning, with my head still a little achy and my nerves stretched tight, I stood in front of Britt's auxiliary room and put my Restorer code into the key-pad next to the door. When the door opened, I slipped inside the room.

I wasn't alone.

Britt turned away from one of the consoles. She studied me for a long moment while I tried to think of some way to explain what I was doing there.

"How are you feeling?" Britt asked quietly.

"I'm fine," I replied. Which had been a lot truer before I'd been caught sneaking into an auxiliary room.

Britt's eyes were far too knowing, but all she did was smile as she walked to the door. Then she hesitated.

"I was about the same age you were when I created my unicorn. My horned horse," she added when I stared at her. "Mine didn't have the elegant equine tail yours did, and it had a beard under its chin." She stroked under her own chin to illustrate. "I'd added that bit because my uncle had a beard like that, and I was fond of him." She smiled again.

When the door opened, she started to step through, then stopped. "We need to do more than what is correct for this world, Willow. We need to do what is *right*. This world…. *This* world is our true Atonement."

When she was gone, I stumbled over to the nearest chair, sat down, and tried to sort out the messages beneath Britt's words.

The horned horse. The unicorn.

One of the projects necessary to qualify for a Restorer team was to create an "oddity" — to take some of the genetic material from the honeycombed chambers and create a new creature that could survive in a natural environment. I suppose the fact that most of the "oddities" couldn't survive outside the lab was supposed to instill in us a realization of the difference between being a Restorer and being the Blessed All who is the Creator. It also showed that there was no room for ego in the work we were choosing to do. When a creature had to be created in order to fill a niche in an ecosystem, it had to be done with care. A world could only tolerate so much ego indulgence before it rebelled.

I had created a horned horse. On the surface, there was nothing else that distinguished it from other equine species, but it was different.

I remember when Britt had been a guest Instructor for one of my classes. She had said that sometimes all the barriers between a person and the Blessed All were flung open. When that happened, it wasn't something that could be described, but it was something that you recognized. And when that happened, what flowed from you was more than what you could point to on the surface, was more than you could knowingly create.

I remember that feeling, that dreamlike quality. It had flowed through me the day I created the horned horse. And when the specimen had been grown and all its data inputted into a computer simulation to observe how it reacted to its environment, I had no explanation for why things were the way they were.

Wherever a unicorn lived, there was Balance. Somehow, its presence kept omnivores from overfeeding in an area so there was always food for every creature that lived within its territory. Predators wouldn't touch it while it lived. When it became old and was ready to return to the Blessed All, predators would follow it at a distance and wait. It would finally choose a spot and lie down. As it took its last breath, the horn would fall off. Then the predators would approach the offered flesh. But before any of them consumed so much as a bite, one of them would dig a hole nearby and bury the horn. It didn't matter what kind of predator it was, whether it traveled in packs or alone. It would bury the horn.

The Scholars and the head Instructors were more than a little startled when they reviewed my project — and some of them were openly upset. But nothing was said to me, and I was accelerated through a couple of levels of study because of that project.

Stev, on the other hand, had almost been thrown out of the program because of his bumbler bee.

It was a bee, a pollinator like other species of bees. Except that it was bigger and looked a little furry. Its wings weren't in proportion to its body size, but it was still able to fly. It "bumbled" from flower to flower, which is why he'd named it a bumbler bee.

The Scholars had grilled him mercilessly because of that bee. What research had he used, where had he gotten it, what sealed files had he accessed. When he insisted that he'd followed the project instructions and had come up with the bumbler bee on his own, they didn't believe him. They acted as though he had found a way to look at the files that contained the Scholars' Secrets — or had done something equally bad. Because of that project, Stev wasn't advanced with the rest of his group. And shortly after that, he switched from the Restorer program to the Restorer's Right Hand program.

No one at that time or since then has ever explained what it was about the bumbler bee that had gotten him into so much trouble.

But it left a scar on Stev's heart that still wasn't healed.

Now, thinking about what Britt had said, I wondered how much she'd had to do with my acceleration through the Restorer program — and how much she'd had to do with making sure Stev hadn't been dismissed from the program altogether.

I sent a message to Stev's personal pad, telling him I had a console and where to meet me.

When he arrived a few minutes later, he looked nervous. "Willow... If we get caught in an auxiliary room..."

"We won't get caught," I said, then added silently, *Britt will see to that.* I couldn't have explained why I was so certain of that, but while I'd been waiting for him, I'd reached two conclusions: Britt knew who had taken responsibility for restoring Balance to the island that had been hers before she had decided to step down as a primary Restorer. And Britt approved.

As soon as I accessed the console, there were three polite, but somewhat impatient, requests that I remove my material from the holding tanks.

"I don't *have* any material," I muttered as I double-checked to make sure the requests were meant for me.

"Willow..." There was a funny catch in Stev's voice.

As we reviewed what was in the holding tanks against the lists we had made, we realized that what we had available was exactly what we needed. Oh, the quantities didn't *quite* match Stev's figures, but close enough. The grass, clover, wildflowers, and groundcover that were at the top of our lists were waiting for us. There was also an unsigned suggestion that we increase the percentage of mature trees.

"Let's think of this as a gift," I said. And, really, that's what it was. By using what was already there, the three days when we couldn't do anything for the land hadn't been lost.

Stev spent the morning working through our lists and sending requests down to the generation tanks for the rest of the "foundation" life-forms — that is, the insects — as well as a variety of shrubs and berry bushes. I spent that time dispersing the seed that was in the holding tanks.

By the time the midday meal came around, a light rain had begun over the island — just enough to give the seeds the water they needed and also to settle them into the earth.

The food slot, which had been a bit whimsical all morning about what it chose to give us, decided to quit altogether when we tried to get a more substantial meal.

"Come on," Stev said, steering me toward the door. "We'll go to one of the food courts."

"But... " I didn't want to go to a food court, especially the one for the older students. It was going to take a while before I could bear to sit in the same room as Dermi.

"Your eyes — and the rest of your head — need a break from staring at that console screen all morning," Stev said firmly.

What was it about Stev that made me the most annoyed with him when he was right?

I began to wonder how much of a break my eyes really needed when we met up with Thanie and Whit outside the older students' food court.

"Why don't we go to the another food court," Whit said as he glanced nervously at the other students who were going through the door. "There's another one a little ways down the corridor."

"We can't go there," Thanie said in a hushed voice. "That one is used by the Restorer teams."

"Well, we can't go into *this* one," Whit snapped.

So we went to the other food court, feeling very self-conscious when we walked through the door. There were a few glances, a few polite smiles. It wasn't that we weren't *allowed* in this food court. It was just that this was a gathering place for the adults.

We got our food and chose a table as far away from everyone else as we could get.

The first bite was enough to remind me that I really was hungry, so I applied myself to my meal. I was halfway through it when Thanie blurted out something that made me lose my appetite.

125

"As soon as she heard you were dismissed from the class project, Dermi asked to handle the trees," Thanie said.

"*Thanie...*" Whit said in a warning voice.

Thanie was too upset to heed the warning. "She used the whole allotment of genetic material to create seedlings."

My fork slipped out of my hand. My stomach began to hurt. "So the deer got their food after all," I said dully.

"She hasn't done a *thing* about bringing the deer population into Balance. By this morning, they'd eaten all the seedlings. Dermi requested another allotment of trees and was told her next allotment wouldn't be available for another 30 days, so now she's in a *major, major* snit." Thanie paused. "And she blames you."

Whit glared at Thanie while Stev said *very* rude things.

"Why does she blame *me*?"

Finally realizing how angry Stev and Whit were at that moment, Thanie hunched into herself.

"She blames you because she's more of a bug-brain than Zerx," Whit finally growled. "If Dermi had bothered to read the project parameters, she would have *known* that tree allotments are given out in 30-day cycles. And what's worse is Fallah, who's supposed to be her best friend, keeps encouraging her rash decisions. The results will put our team score right into the waste recycler, but it will sure make Fallah's individual score look good compared to everyone else's."

"Excuse me," I said, pushing away from the table. "I — Excuse me."

When Stev started to rise, I put my hand on his shoulder to keep him in his chair.

As I headed for the door, I glanced to my left.

Zashi was watching me, a concerned look on his face.

I tried to smile in greeting. I couldn't quite manage it, so I hurried out of the room.

I sat in the auxiliary room, glad to be alone for a while. I told myself over and over that the student project was no longer my concern, that *those* trees were no longer *my* trees, and that I had other work to do — other land to restore to Balance.

I understood that Balance was give and take, that life-forms lived...and life-forms died. I understood that some life-forms became extinct, not because of carelessness or indulgence, but because their time in the world had come to an end. When extinction was a natural part of the ebb and flow of the world, something else would come along to fill that space. It was when a life-form ceased to exist before its time was done that a hole was left in the world. That was when Balance itself could become extinct.

By the time Stev returned from the food court, I had pretty much convinced myself that one allotment of trees used foolishly wouldn't *really* make any difference to this world.

That night, one of the generation tanks failed completely, and there was nothing any of the techs could do to save the life-forms that had been growing inside it.

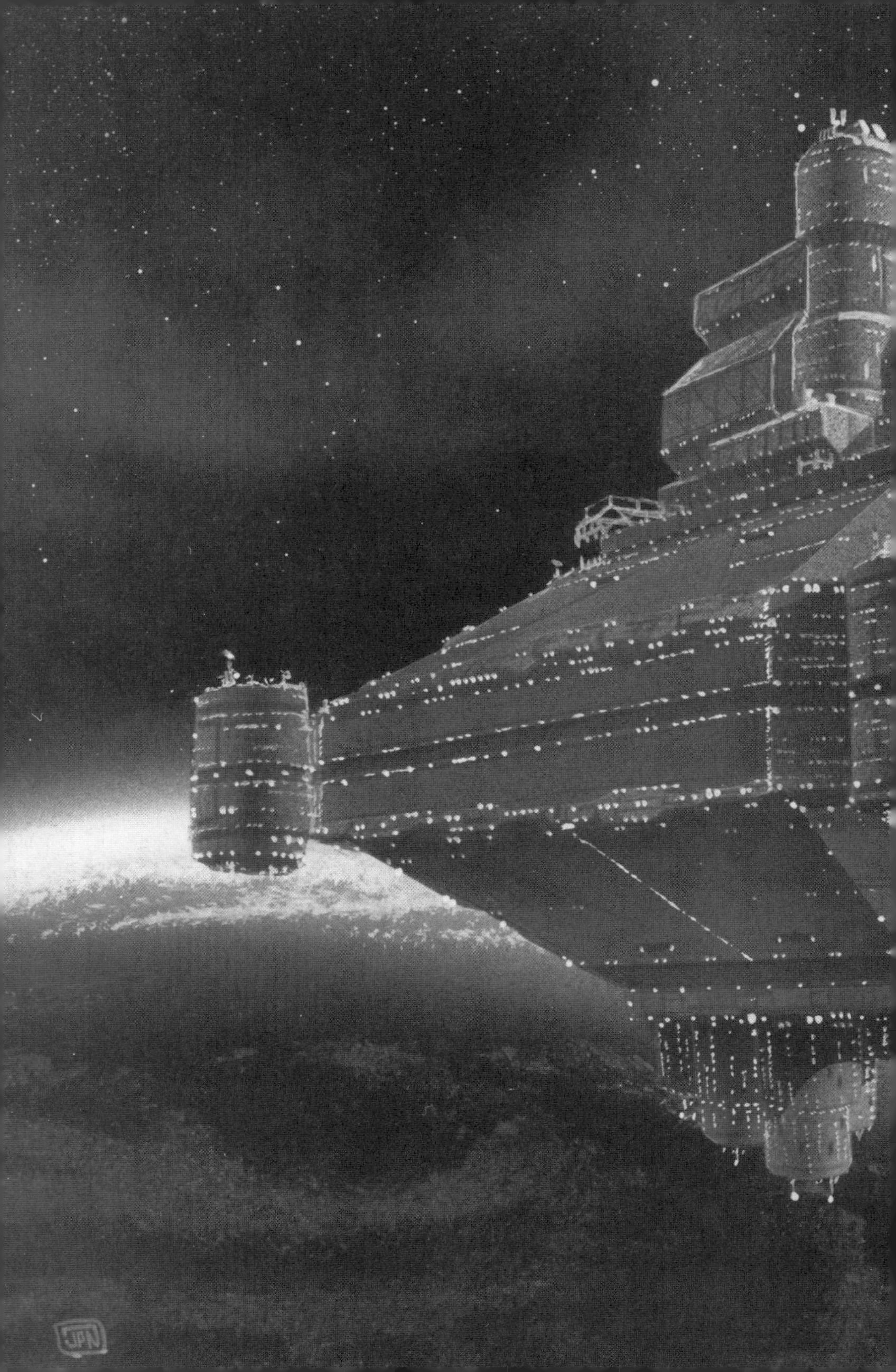
JPN

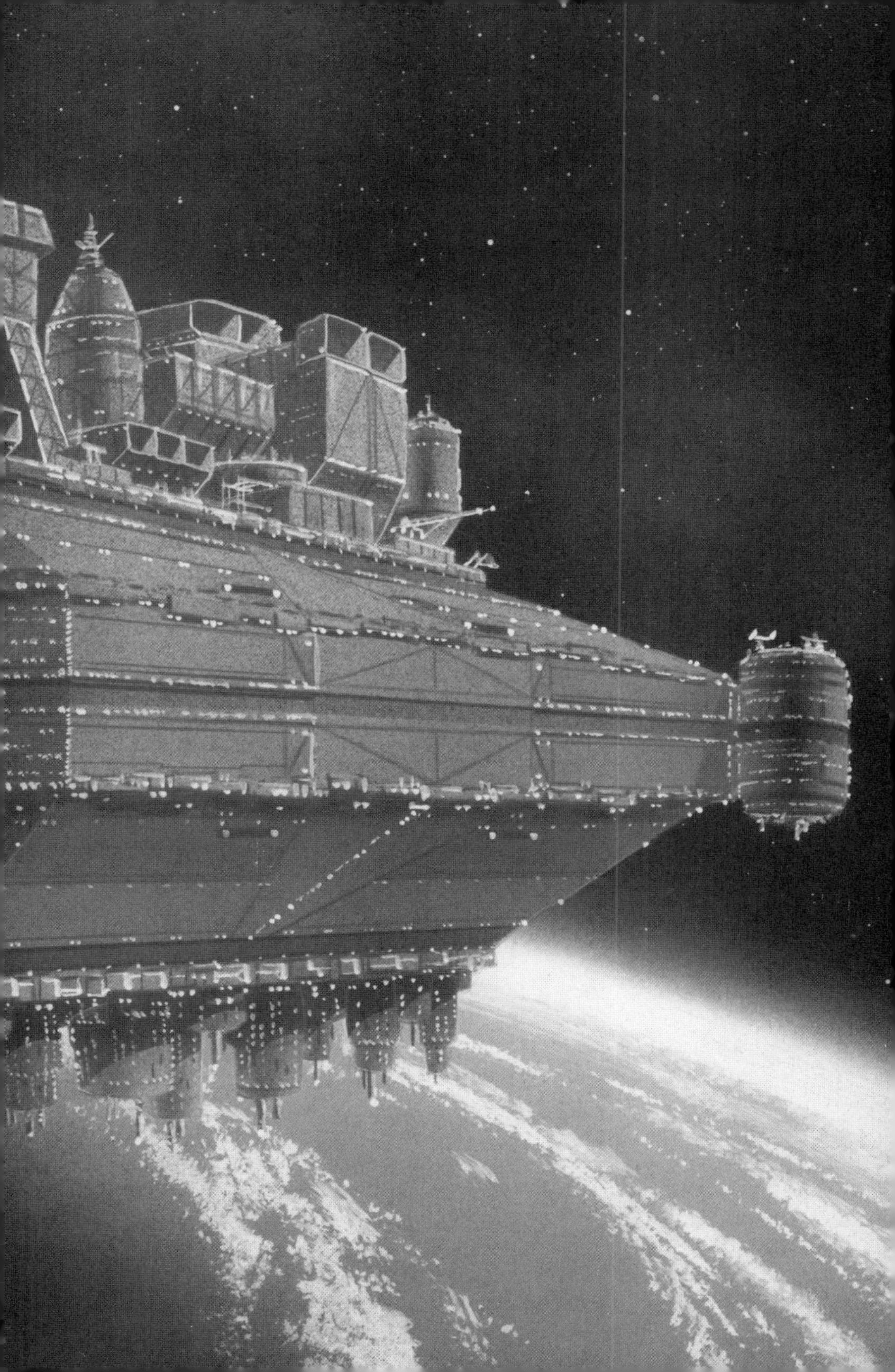

6

Over the next few days, we worked. The grass seed we had initially dispersed had sprouted and was growing well. Some of the flowers had begun to sprout. Following my directives, Stev began accelerating some new plants to the point where they were in flower.

During that time, two more generation tanks developed problems. The techs, who were now extremely vigilant, immediately sounded the alarm. The engineers were able to stop the system failure in those tanks, but a memo came through from the techs strongly recommending that those two tanks shouldn't be used at more than 50% capacity.

A lot of ants could be created in a tank that could only function at half capacity, but that recommendation would have a serious effect when it came to larger life-forms.

During that same time, the problem with the heating system had spread from the corridors into the living quarters. My room would change within the space of an hour from freezing cold to being hot enough to make me sweat.

Stev didn't say a thing about the heating system or the problems with the generation tanks, but I knew what he was thinking.

Our city-ships are very, very old. Our people had been wandering through space for many, many of our generations. There were spaceports that belonged to other races where we could stop and make repairs once in a while. But we couldn't build new ships to take the place of the old ones because the generation tanks wouldn't work in any ship but the ones they had been built for, and we no longer had the skill to make new tanks.

It was as if, for one brief point in our people's history, we had been given the gift of knowledge to create the piece of technology that would give our people a chance to make Atonement. Once the ships, and the generation tanks, were built, that knowledge faded away, never to return.

Our engineers could maintain and repair the tanks, and they understood, *in theory*, how to build them. But they simply couldn't build one the size and complexity of the original tanks. The engineers have been trying for generations. Sometimes a very small tank was built and actually worked, but it could only produce one small specimen at a time. The results of trying to grow anything larger than a rabbit were ghastly. And trying to grow more than one specimen of *anything* in one of those tanks...

Sometimes one healthy specimen survived. Sometimes.

Everything has a life span. Even a ship.

Slowly, one-by-one, our city-ships have been dying.

We seldom meet another ship that belongs to our people. When we do, we travel together for a while. These rare meetings are the only way for us to bring new blood into our population. Sometimes people want to leave their own city-ship because of some unhappiness in their lives. Some people leave because they fall in love, and one partner is willing to give up family and friends to be with the other.

It takes courage and deep feelings to make such a choice because the chances are very slim that they'll ever meet up again with the city-ship that had once been home.

And then there are the survivors.

I was barely old enough at the time to remember when our ship picked up a weak distress call from a sister ship. It took weeks to reach it, despite the fact that we had headed for it with all possible speed.

When we got there, we noticed that the small shuttle ships were missing, and there was some speculation that a few people had tried to use them to escape. But shuttle ships, which were capable of transporting us between one ship and another, were not meant for long journeys. There had been no world within range that they could have reached.

The people of that ship had done what they could. What little power was left had been channeled to the honeycomb chambers that held the genetic material — and it had been channeled to the cryotubes. These tubes usually stored specimens that had been carefully grown so that fresh genetic material could be added to the honeycomb chambers to replace material that had become too old to be viable.

When the team from our ship had gone over to look for any sign of life, they had found the two hundred cryotubes filled with children. Only eight of those tubes were still functioning. Those eight children were brought to our ship.

One of them was Stev.

So I didn't offer him assurances neither of us could believe. We just did the work while we could.

I discovered the problem in the honeycomb chambers when I put in my request for bees. A few minutes after I sent the request, the console chimed that I had an urgent message.

IF NOT USED IMMEDIATELY, THERE MAY NOT BE ENOUGH VIABLE MATERIAL AVAILABLE TO PRODUCE REQUESTED NUMBER OF SPECIMENS.

Muttering to myself, I spent close to the next hour working my way through the command series that would allow me to view the honeycomb chambers that stored the genetic material.

Obviously, there had been a mistake. Somehow the computer had misread my request. Bees weren't some exotic species. They were *bees*. They went *buzz*, they helped pollinate plants as they gathered pollen for food, they made honey. And I had *checked* the amount of available genetic material just two days ago to make sure there would be enough, since I figured every Restorer team would want to disperse bees.

When I finally got to view the honeycomb chambers that held the genetic material for bees, I just stared at the screen. A shiver went through me — a shiver that grew and grew until I began to shake.

The honeycomb chambers had a color code. Green chambers held genetic material. White meant the chamber had been emptied, the material had been completely used. Pink meant the computer was picking up a problem within that cell that could damage the material. Red was a major alert that the genetic material was in danger. Black meant the material within that cell had died.

The area designated for bees was spotted with black and red cells. As I watched, two red cells turned black, and several pink cells changed to red.

With my heart pounding, I keyed in a Priority Urgent message warning every Restorer team that there was a problem with the honeycomb chambers. I also sent the message to the techs' consoles at the generation tanks. At that point, I didn't care who knew I had a Restorer code or that I was handling the island. The teams had to be warned.

As soon as I sent that message, I sent a Priority Urgent to Stev, who had gone down to the generation tanks to oversee the transfer of genetic material to start the field mice we would add to the meadows. I told him to put a hold on the mice and draw *all* the genetic material available for bees and get it into a generation tank.

A minute later, as I watched more green cells change to pink, I got back the query: *??*

DON'T ARGUE. JUST DO IT!!! I sent that message twice.

Stev didn't respond.

"Hurry, Stev," I whispered, clenching my hands so hard they began to cramp. "Please hurry."

More pink cells turned red. Some red cells turned black.

Then, one by one, the red cells turned white. The pink cells turned white. Finally, the green cells turned white.

I finally managed to take a deep breath — and realized I was crying.

There was a strong possibility that the material in the red cells wouldn't be able to create healthy bees anymore. Stev, being Stev, would have put that material in another tank so that it wouldn't contaminate the rest if it was no longer viable.

Whatever bees we managed to grow would have to be shared among the Restorer teams that needed them. There wouldn't be enough. We would need another pollinator.

I got a cup of tea from the food slot. I thought it over carefully — and followed my intuition.

When I did a little checking, I discovered that someone had taken Stev's little "oddity" and had been carefully growing more specimens from it. There were several dozen cells filled with its genetic material.

I waited until Stev sent a message that he was returning to the auxiliary room.

Then I sent another Priority message to the techs overseeing the generation tanks.

I was the Restorer for the island. I was the only one who chose what was given to that land — and I was the only one who would be held responsible for that choice.

Before Stev arrived, I got back confirmation from one of the techs.

When the next generation tank became available, it would be growing Stev's bumbler bees.

When I got home, Mother was crying her heart out and holding on to Father as if he were her entire world.

"There was nothing we could have done, Rista," Father said quietly as he rubbed her back, trying to soothe her. "Even if we had known about the problem before today, there was nothing we could have done. Those species aren't right for this world. They would have always been out of Balance."

"I know. I know. But... Jeromi... *Extinct.*"

"We don't know that. There might be another ship — "

Father saw me at that moment and didn't continue. It had been a long time since we had heard from another city-ship. There was no certainty that there *were* any others out there anymore.

I saw the conflict in his eyes. There were two people he loved who were hurting, and he wasn't sure which one of us needed him more.

I smiled at him and went to my room — not because I didn't need the comfort or the hug, but because Mother

136

needed him more right now and deserved to have him all to herself for a little while.

Because Mother was one of those people who had given up everything they had known out of love for another person.

I took my hologram down from its shelf and turned it on, watched it for a while.

An overloaded circuit had been the reason why the warnings had never reached the techs' consoles. Oh, they'd gotten erratic warnings once in a while, but it was always during times when material was being removed from the cells to go into the generation tanks. Since all the self-tests showed no problem with the system, they concluded that the warnings were a computer error.

It still wasn't clear *why* my accessing the information at that moment triggered the warning circuit, but my sounding the alarm produced an awful scramble in the tank rooms. In fact, my request for bumbler bees was the last confirmed request for the rest of the day.

It was while the techs were checking out the system that they discovered just how much genetic material had already been destroyed. Fortunately, none of the species that no longer existed were vital to this world, and some couldn't have lived on the planet under any condition, but that didn't make it any better.

"Extinct" was the most terrible word we knew.

And if we were the last surviving city-ship, it was a word that would apply to us very soon.

7

A couple of days later, while Stev and I were eating the midday meal in the Restorers' food court, Whit showed up. He got a plate of food and then just sat and stared at it for several minutes.

"Thanie resigned from the program," he said abruptly. "So did I."

"*What?*" I put my glass down before I dropped it.

"What happened?" Stev asked sharply.

"The… The songbirds were being destroyed from every direction. They were starving, and there were so many predators after them, the ones who weren't actually killed as prey were dying from fright and exhaustion. She just couldn't stand watching it anymore. So this morning, she sent in a request to have all the remaining songbirds transferred out of the area. The approval came in about an hour before the midday break. When the rest of the team realized what she'd done, you should have heard the way they shrieked about it. Dermi and Fallah were still yelling at her when she keyed in her resignation, shut down her console, and left."

"What about you, Whit?" I asked.

His eyes were bright with tears. "What's the point of putting up with bug-brains like Zerx and Dermi and Fallah — or even Benj, for that matter? The ship is dying. Everyone knows it even if no one will admit it. There's no reason to do this since it's not going to make any difference."

His voice had risen to the point where several people around us had turned to look at us with not-too-pleased expressions on their faces.

"Not the Restorer teams," he said, his voice dropping back to normal. "I don't mean them. They're doing *real* work and they *are* making a difference to this world. But there's no reason for me to keep gritting my teeth and trying to work with the rest of those *people* in order to earn my qualification. There's no future in it." He tried to smile at a joke that was, in its honesty, obscene.

None of us finished our meals. Stev took Whit off to talk for a while. I went over to Thanie's and ended up saying useless things while she cried.

It was a couple of hours before I got back to the auxiliary room. Out of habit, I called up the screen that listed the species that were now in the area we were restoring. Several names popped up on the screen with the "new species" symbol next to them.

I stared at the screen. Birds? *Birds?* I hadn't *requested* birds yet. There weren't supposed to *be* any birds yet.

I keyed in the command for the computer to locate and provide a planetside view of one of these birds.

There it was, a little sparrow that was barely able to hold on to the branch of a sapling oak tree.

"What's going on here? The Restorer screen is supposed to *prevent* things like this from happening," I muttered as I started to key in a demand to remove those birds. Granted, in a few more days, I intended to request birds from the generation tanks, but...

That's when it occurred to me to check my messages *before* I sent that demand to the tank techs.

There was a directive accepting a transfer of song-birds. The directive had a Restorer code that wasn't mine. It also had very specific instructions about the placement of the birds. They had been scattered over the several thousand acres of land that Stev and I were restoring. Despite being added prematurely, the birds really wouldn't be consuming more food than the land could provide.

Which wasn't the point, I assured myself as I muttered my way through the directive. Those birds shouldn't *be* there until *I* decided they should be there.

And then I got to the end of the directive. The Restorer code was repeated. Under it was simply — *Britt.*

I sat back, no longer sure what to think.

I checked my other messages — which I hadn't bothered to do since I hadn't expected any to come through on this console — and found the transfer request. It had been an open request. That meant it had been sent to every Restorer code the computer recognized, and anyone who wanted any of those birds could request them to be sent to the area that person was restoring.

Britt, for whatever reason, had initiated the transfer of the birds to the island.

No. Not "for whatever reason." They were living creatures. The person who had requested the transfer had done so in order to save them. In a few more days, I would have requested the same species. And I still would in order to bring the numbers up to a viable population.

But I think Britt, who sometimes understood too well, knew exactly what my decision would have been if I'd read the transfer request when it first came in.

Just as she understood exactly how Thanie would feel if she knew her beloved songbirds were safe with me.

8

"Willow? Where are you going?"

Glancing over my shoulder, I saw Thanie hurrying to catch up with me.

"I have some … stuff … to do," I said lamely as I continued walking toward the auxiliary room.

"Can I help?" Thanie said. "It's just… Well, I thought since you didn't have class either…"

The entire walk was filled with her unfinished sentences, but I understood the gist of it. Thanie didn't want to sit home doing nothing while there was an entire world aching to be restored. She had no idea how I had been filling my days since I'd been dismissed from the class project and probably figured that two people doing nothing might create more of an illusion of doing *something*.

I was still trying to figure out what kind of excuse to give her when we reached the auxiliary room. As it turned out, I didn't need an excuse. As I approached the auxiliary room from one direction with Thanie, Stev approached it from the other direction with Whit, who had the same lost look that Thanie had.

I looked at Stev. Stev looked at me.

"Well," I said. "Four can do more than two." I put my code into the keypad. The door opened. "Let's get to work."

"Willow…" Thanie said as she followed me into the room. "Students aren't supposed to be in auxiliary rooms."

"We're not students anymore, remember?" I replied as Stev and I started opening our consoles. "Thanie, why don't you take that console." I indicated the one immediately on my left. "Whit, you take the one next to Stev."

Whit looked around the small room. "You got permission to do a special project?" he asked, looking hopeful. "Could I — " He glanced at Thanie. "Could we help? Not for credit or anything."

That made me pause. I looked at Thanie.

This wasn't about getting credit. This wasn't about getting points on a score — or even getting formally qualified. They just wanted to do the work.

Stev was the one who broke the silence. "If you're going to be here," he said dryly, "we didn't expect you to just sit there and play with your fingers."

"So ... what's the project?" Whit asked.

Stev and I braced ourselves to catch them as I called up the screen that showed the entire project. We didn't want to start the day with a trip to sick bay because someone hit the floor.

Whit and Thanie just stared at the screen, their mouths hanging open.

"Blessed All," Whit finally said. "You've done that much by yourselves?"

Pain and fury flashed in his eyes for a moment before he regained control. He was seeing the difference between what a *real* team, even if it consisted of only two people, could accomplish compared to what was done by one that was a team in name only.

"We've done that much," I said, feeling the pleasure of that accomplishment warm me. "And we've got a lot more to do. Thanie, you've got the birds."

"Willow..."

Since I was already at my console, transferring the data to *her* console, she took her seat. When she looked at the number of birds, tears filled her eyes. She knew where they had come from.

She sniffed a couple of times and then firmed up. "You don't have any hawks or falcons."

"They'll have to be added...along with the other bird species that are designated as being appropriate for this ecosystem."

I watched her take that in. She would be handling *all* of the birds — and that included the ones that would eat the songbirds.

She closed her eyes for a moment, took a deep breath, and nodded.

In a land that had Balance, Thanie would be able to accept the give and take of life.

While Thanie and Whit spent the next couple of hours acquainting themselves with the project, Stev continued to work through the lists of species we would need and I went through the messages that had been sent to this console.

Most of them were from the Restorers, basically offering understated praise for saving the bees. They also carefully indicated that they would like some of the bees if any were available.

Since I had initiated the order to grow the bees, I was entitled to keep as many as I wanted or needed. If I kept all of them, I would have a full population of bees for the island, but everyone else would have to scramble to find something else to take the bees' place in the ecosystems they were restoring. So we would share them.

Besides, I had the bumblers, which no one but the tank techs knew about yet.

144

The next message was from a tank tech informing me that all the genetic material for the bumblers had been placed in a generation tank and was being grown at the same slow acceleration rate that Stev had ordered for the other bees.

The message after that was from another tank tech informing me that the bees would be ready for dispersal in twenty hours. That message was copied to Stev.

The last message was from Zashi, who warmly praised my quick action concerning the bees and then gently offered his assistance. If I were willing to release the equivalent of two small hives — queens, drones, and workers — he would personally oversee using them as the genetic base to create more bees.

That was a tough decision to make. The generation tanks didn't require large amounts of material to start growing another specimen, but it seemed unfair to create something and then turn around and use it to create more of its kind without ever giving it a chance to live. But I was also aware that two queen bees would provide enough material to create close to fifty more queen bees. And fifty hives, that could then produce more bees on their own, would go a lot further toward giving every Restorer team starter hives.

I keyed in a message to Zashi taking him up on his offer. I copied the message to Stev, with an additional note that listed the Restorer teams who had requested bees. He would see that each team got an equal number of bees — or as close to it as possible.

By the time we were ready for a midday break, Thanie was bubbling over with enthusiasm. "Just wait until — "

"*No.*" I blocked the door. "This project is need-to-know *only*, Thanie. It doesn't get discussed with anyone who isn't working on it."

I knew she wanted to rub Dermi's and Fallah's noses in the fact that we were working on a major project, but there was still a chance that we could be shut down if this came to *too* many people's attention.

I saw her struggle with the disappointment. That was my real reservation about having Thanie work on this project. When pushed, she tended to blurt out confidential information in order to regain some emotional ground.

"What about my parents?" Thanie finally asked. "Can I tell — "

"They aren't need-to-know when it comes to this project," Stev said firmly.

Whit shifted uneasily. "You *do* have approval for this, don't you? I mean, you didn't ... lift ... the Restorer code or anything?"

"I have approval," I replied. "And there is a primary Restorer who is ... aware ... of the work."

That was enough for Whit and, apparently, Thanie.

Stev just gave me a searching look. After getting a message from Zashi, it wasn't hard for him to figure out who the Restorer was who was aware of our work. But I wasn't prepared to tell even Stev just *how* aware Britt was of our work.

And I wasn't going to start wondering *why* she was so interested in what I would do with the land.

9

A couple of days later, while the four of us were eating what the food slots in the Restorers' food court had decided to offer for a midday meal, Zashi stopped by our table.

"The new bees are growing very nicely," he said, smiling at me. "They'll be distributed tomorrow." Then he gave me a speculative look. "I just came from the tank rooms. One of the techs, since I was assisting you with the bees, didn't see any harm in mentioning that your other specimens were nicely grown and ready for dispersal. I believe you'll find a message to that effect when you get back to work. I gather you want to give them a chance to prove themselves before offering them to anyone else?"

"Yes," I said, feeling my smile become brittle. "That's it exactly."

"I don't think you'll find that to be an issue — at least, not with any Restorer." He lifted his hand in farewell and went to join friends at another table.

"What other specimens?" Stev asked.

"I'll explain later," I muttered, not daring to look at him.

There had been a blend of amusement and sympathy in Zashi's eyes before he left us that clearly told me he knew as well as I did who was going to make an issue out of this.

When we got back to the auxiliary room, Stev read the message waiting for us and threw a fit.

"How could you?" he shouted. "How *could* you? I have spent *years* trying to put that behind me."

"They're pollinators. They're viable. They work in this ecosystem. We *need* them," I shouted back.

"They *aren't* viable. They *don't* fit! The Scholars and Instructors made that very clear when they reviewed the project."

"*I'm* the Restorer for this team, and *I* say they fit!" If there wasn't so much hurt under the anger, I could have punched him for being so stubborn. "They're *bees*, Stev, and *we need bees*."

He turned away from me.

Whit quietly cleared his throat. "Uh ... Thanie and I have some ... stuff ... to do. We'll be back in a little while." Taking a firm grip on Thanie's arm, he dragged her out of the room.

I barely noticed them leave.

"They'll chew on you for this, Willow," Stev said bitterly.

"Let them try." I waited until he turned to face me. "I'll put our work up against *any* Restorer team. I don't know why the Scholars and Instructors made such a fuss over the bumblers. I don't care why they did. They were *wrong*, Stev." I was so angry at that point, I started to cry. "They were *wrong*."

"Willow..." Stev put his arms around me. "Don't cry, Willow. Please don't cry."

148

I did my best to stop, not because I was ready to, but mostly because seeing me cry made Stev feel helpless.

Stev sighed. "I guess no one will really notice a handful of bumblers."

Obviously, he had only gotten far enough into the message to read "bumbler bees" and hadn't actually taken in the *quantity* of specimens that were ready for dispersal. Once he had, hopefully he, too, would start wondering why someone had taken the time and trouble to produce that much genetic material for an "oddity" that had no value.

Now there was just the little problem of dispersing the bumblers. As much as I cared about Stev and would trust him without question at any other time, I couldn't be sure he wouldn't dump the bumblers under six inches of water somewhere if he was the one handling the dispersal. Since I'd ordered *all* the genetic material for the bumblers to be drawn from the honeycomb chambers, if Stev did something rash out of some misguided idea of saving the rest of the project, there wouldn't be any way of starting over and producing bumblers again.

Wiping my eyes with my sleeve, I checked my console for messages while Stev slumped in his chair.

There was one message — from Zashi. All it said was, *Bumblers??*

Thank the Blessed All for Zashi. He was offering to handle the dispersal. Stev would have had another fit if I had asked Whit to take care of the bumblers, but there wasn't much he could say when a primary Restorer's Right Hand offered to handle it.

Yes, please, I answered.

A few minutes after Thanie and Whit returned, a message came in from Zashi, copied to Stev, thanking me for allowing him to participate a little and make use of his skills.

I busily avoided Stev's stare until he settled back to work.

And I smiled when, much later that evening after Stev had already gone home, I watched a bumbler land on a flower.

<u>10</u>

We worked as long as we could and as hard as we could. It still wasn't enough.

Every day there was a circuit failure in another system. The engineers would just get one repaired and two more would go down. The tank techs were sending messages every morning, warning the Restorer teams about continued failures in the honeycomb chambers and which species were threatened. And every Restorer team was using the generation tanks at full acceleration now, even though there was more risk that a fully accelerated specimen might have less reproductive capability.

We just wanted to get as much life down on the planet as possible before a vital system in the ship failed — like life support or the ability to maintain orbit.

I was alone in the auxiliary room. I'd sent Whit and Thanie home because there was nothing else that could be done at the moment, and Stev had gone to check out something in the tank rooms before getting some sleep.

I was tired enough that I had slipped into that state of waking dreams. I stared at the screen in front of me, not really seeing it anymore.

Every link in the chain of survival had to be built in the right order and at the right time. That's what we'd been taught in every Restorer class. That idea was fine when there was more than enough time, but it wasn't going to work now. If I waited until I reached a particular link in the chain at this point, the genetic material might not still exist when I needed it. But if I *didn't* follow procedure, I risked the Balance the island now had.

As I stared at the screen, I felt a surge of energy flow through my body. I sat up. I really *looked* at the planet-side picture that was on the screen.

For several minutes, I watched a spider build a web.

Not a *chain* of survival — a *web of life*. A link was only connected to the links on either side of it. But a web... Each strand affected *every* strand in the overall scheme of the web, but in the end, there was Balance.

With the image of a web held firmly in my mind, I looked over my lists again.

I might not be able to send enough of each animal and plant down to the planet in time to assure that each species would be able to sustain itself, but for a shining moment, a part of that island would be fully restored and there would be Balance.

<u>11</u>

The next morning, Whit and Thanie looked very confused as they reviewed the list of species I had requested from the generation tanks. Stev looked very concerned.

I knew what he was thinking: that I'd been working too hard and something inside me had snapped.

There was no way I could explain it to him, but something inside me hadn't snapped, it was now wide open. Balance flowed through me in a way it never had before. I was no longer following the rules that had been laid down for us in class. I was the Restorer — and I finally understood what that really meant.

"Willow…" Stev said. Before he could go on, the door opened. Britt and Zashi stepped inside.

Britt's eyes met mine and held.

She had been waiting for this moment, had been wondering if it would come.

"Would you like some help?" she asked.

I just smiled.

Britt, Zashi, and I slipped into working together as if we'd always done so. After a couple of hours, Stev was almost in stride with us. Whit and Thanie were bewildered by the change in the project's direction and a little dazed at suddenly working in such close quarters with the most respected Restorer and Restorer's Right Hand on the ship.

At midday, Britt and Zashi excused themselves, saying they had other commitments during the afternoon.

I thanked them both — and was greatly relieved when they assured me they would be back the next morning.

As they were about to leave, I overheard Zashi say to Stev, "Give yourself some time. You'll get used to working with someone like her."

12

Later that evening, when I had finally gone home to get some sleep, I found a list that had been sent to my personal computer pad. I didn't need to be told that it had come from the Scholars' secret files. I also didn't need anyone to tell me that the sender had taken great care to make sure access to that file couldn't be traced to me.

It was a long list. A terrible list. At the top was the heading, *Lab Specimens Are The Only Specimens Now Available.*

I read the list. Wolf, crow, hawk, falcon. Salmon, dolphin, fox, panda. Bison, zebra, elk, tiger. Nightingale, otter, cobra, seal. The list went on and on. If I compared this list to the list of species that were suitable for this world and were waiting in the honeycomb chambers as genetic material, they would match. I was certain of it.

The next part of the list was much, much longer. Its heading simply said *Extinct.*

Near the bottom of that list, I found the reason why the Scholars had been so upset with Stev — and why they had suspected him of accessing their secret files. The entry said *Bumblebee.*

Stev had re-created a creature that had become extinct before its time in the world was done. If the Scholars hadn't slapped him down to the point that he would never be willing to try again, who knows what other creatures he might have given back to the world?

The last part of the list said *Myths.* The very last entry was the unicorn.

I looked at that entry for a long time. Then I deleted the list because the underlying message, and the reason the list had been sent, hadn't been meant for anyone but me.

13

We worked for another month while the ship failed around us. Whit had continued to disperse grass seed and wildflowers over the rest of the island whenever we could get them. Thanie dispersed seeds to build young woodlands while I planted the saplings that would give those woodlands an anchor. Britt added the deer. She had insisted on using the genetic material that was still available instead of transferring animals from another location. I was grateful to her for understanding that I could never have felt impartial about the deer if they had originally been Dermi's.

We had six breeds of horses. There were cows and sheep, hawks and falcons, foxes and hares, mice and owls. We had salmon and trout in the streams, and frogs lived among the cattails and water lilies in the ponds. There were woodlands and shrubs and meadows. We planted fields of oats and barley as well as plots of every other vegetable the land would support. Parsley and thyme were among the herbs that had taken root. There was a small population of every kind of creature that belonged to this land. And we had the plant life to support it all.

In that one portion of the island, we had Balance.

We hugged each other. We cheered. We laughed until we cried.

We had Balance.

Over time, the plants and animals would spread out over the rest of the island and grow in number.

We wouldn't see it. But that didn't matter.

And then, the next evening, Stev told me something that changed everything.

Stev waited until the others had left for the day. Then he put his hands on my shoulders.

"Willow…" It took him a moment to try again. "Willow, I was talking to one of the tank techs today. In order to try to save the specimens that are needed to restore this world, they're going to start cutting the power to the rest of the honeycomb chambers. All the genetic material stored in those cells will die."

I felt a deep sorrow, but I understood the necessity. We wouldn't be traveling to any other worlds. We had to do what we could for this one.

"That includes the student projects," Stev said softly.

It took me a moment to understand.

"The unicorns," I whispered.

"I'm so sorry, Willow."

I closed my eyes, and tried to wait out the pain.

"They can't die," I said. *Not again.*

I don't know why that thought filled my head, but once it was there, there was nothing else.

Turning away from Stev, I worked my way through the commands that would show me the honeycomb chamber that held the genetic material for my unicorns. When I found it, I couldn't say anything.

There was just enough material to create a small but viable population of unicorns. But if even one cell was lost…

Then I remembered something else. It took a few minutes more before I found it.

Half of the cells containing the genetic material had turned black.

"If we made them all weaned foals, there would be just enough material for a small population. And my adult unicorns would look after them along with the other foals."

"We can't do it, Willow," he said, his voice thick with regret. "We can't put a species on this world that doesn't belong here."

I knew what he was thinking. I had saved his bumbler bees, and he had to be the one to tell me that I couldn't save something that I had loved ever since I'd seen that one specimen that had been grown in the generation tanks.

He cared — and I loved him for it.

He was also wrong.

"They don't belong here, Willow."

I smiled sadly. "Yes, they do. This is where they came from, Stev. This is their home."

His eyes widened. He stared at me as if he'd never seen me before. Then he looked at the screen and frowned. "I wonder why they had put the genetic material into two different honeycomb chambers."

"Those are Britt's unicorns."

He seemed to have trouble breathing for a minute. "Blessed All," he whispered.

I waited.

He took a deep breath. Blew it out. "I'd better get down to the tanks and do this myself. You stay here and send me the cell numbers. That way I won't have to go through any of the tech consoles where this might get traced."

When he reached the door, he paused and looked back at me. "Zashi was right. It will take a bit of time to get used to working with you."

14

Since they were the only ones available at the time, Stev used the two generation tanks that were working at half capacity. He set them at full growth acceleration so that they would be available again as fast as possible.

When a fully operational tank became available, he insisted on placing some of my unicorns in it.

I couldn't argue with him. The speed at which the cells were changing from green to pink to red to black was terrifying.

The techs weren't interested in what he was doing. They were scrambling to take care of what they could for the Restorer teams, and were happy that he was willing to do his own work.

Whenever he could, he jumped in and filled another generation tank before the techs could put other material into it. As soon as a tank finished the growth process, I issued the command code to send the unicorns down to the island.

I don't think either of us really slept for days.

Finally, the moment came when Stev placed the last surviving material into the generation tanks.

A couple of days after that, we sent the last of the unicorns down to the island.

The day after that, an angry group of Scholars and Instructors showed up at the auxiliary room door.

15

Thanie was wracked with guilt and kept apologizing in between bouts of tears.

We'd warned her, again and again. But a couple of verbal jabs from Dermi and Fallah were all it had taken for her to lash out and tell them about the special project.

Of course, Dermi and Fallah immediately went to the Head Instructor and told *him* everything — including the fact that there were bumbler bees on the island. Which is what brought in the Scholars.

Stev and I were still groggy from lack of sleep. We were just sitting at our consoles, drinking tea and trying to wake up enough to function, when Whit and Thanie were herded into the room, followed by the primary Scholars and the Head Instructor. Behind *them* came Britt and Zashi.

Stev jumped to his feet. A younger person was supposed to rise whenever a Scholar or Instructor came into the room.

I remained seated. I sipped my tea and stared them down.

That made them furious. And, for some reason, nervous.

Accusations filled the room. I had deceived my Instructor by falsifying the information when I made the request for the special project. A *student* would never have been given a restoration project the size of the island. I had deceived the tank techs into believing that I was a qualified Restorer entitled to the special considerations I was given. I had *lied* to them in order to remove unsuitable genetic material.

During this harangue, Britt watched me.

I just sat there, drinking my tea.

When the yelling finally wound down, the Head Instructor said, "Well? What do you have to say to us?"

"Nothing," I replied calmly. "I have nothing to say to you. I do not answer to you."

"Oh?" said the Head Scholar. "If not to us, then who *do* you answer to?"

"The Blessed All."

They stared at me. Britt pressed a hand over her mouth.

I smiled at her. "I have something to show you."

I keyed in the coordinates and requested a planetside picture.

A meadow, on the edge of a woodland. Butterflies flitted by. Birds flew from tree to tree. A bumbler went from one flower to another, doing its duty.

A minute passed. Two minutes.

Then, from among the trees came a white unicorn mare. Beside her were two fillies. One of the fillies had a beard under her chin.

Tears filled Britt's eyes. Then she started to laugh — a joyous, heart-deep laugh. "I knew you were the one. I knew."

"You took a risk," I said. "You could have gotten more of them out in time. We saved what we could."

163

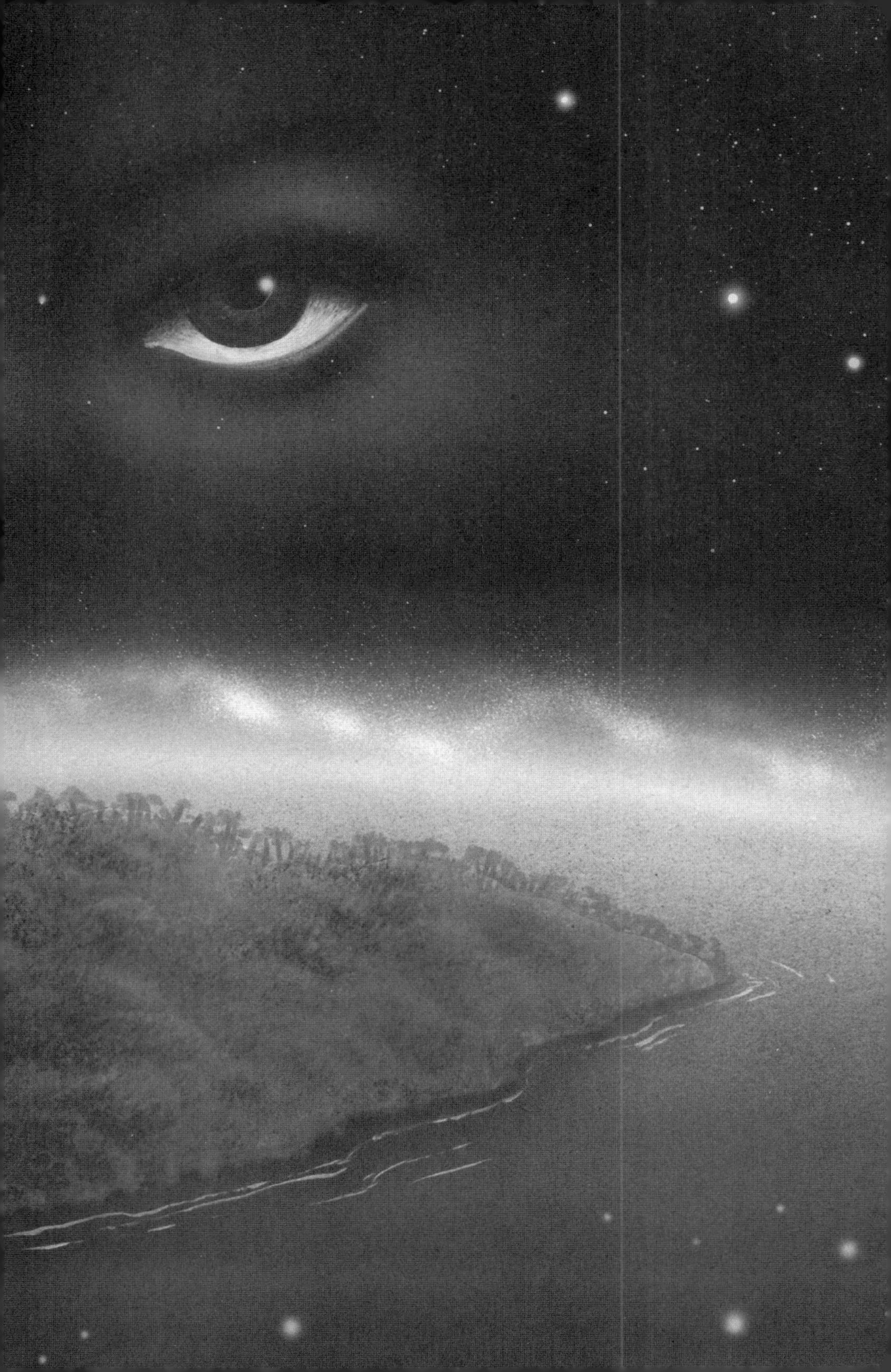

Britt smiled at me. Zashi's eyes began to twinkle.

Somewhere — perhaps on the part of the student island that hadn't been designated for the students — there were more of Britt's unicorns. If I had failed this last test, there might not have been enough of them to survive. Britt had been willing to take that risk...because she needed the certainty of this last test.

"Willow is my successor," Britt said. She walked out of the room.

Zashi winked at me, smiled at Stev, and followed her.

The Scholars and the Head Instructor turned pale. Without another word, they left, taking Whit and Thanie with them.

It had come to me last night, just before I fell asleep for a few hours. All of the other Restorers were referred to as *a* Restorer. Britt was referred to as *the* Restorer. She answered to no one but the Blessed All — because Britt was always in Balance.

And because Britt would not do just what was correct, she would do what was right.

16

Tomorrow we are going to attempt to land our ship on the planet's surface.

The engineers have reluctantly admitted that it's *possible*, but they aren't sure we can do it. But if we *don't* try it, we won't survive another month out in space. If we succeed, we'll gain a few more years to continue our work before the ship dies completely.

The Scholars, of course, argued against it.

It was Britt who decided.

I've wondered if her decision would have been different if I hadn't saved the unicorns. If, without someone to take her place as *the* Restorer, she would have let her own people die rather than risk the world that is still slowly being restored to Balance.

I think I know the answer. That is why I will never ask her.

We have lived in a world made of metal, wandering the galaxy and restoring worlds to Balance because we have to make Atonement for something we had done long ago.

Now we have a chance to feel the earth beneath our feet, to feel the wind on our skin, to smell the wildflowers, to press our hands against the bark of a tree. We have a chance to live as one strand in the web. And we can never afford to forget that we *are* only one strand.

I don't think my people will ever again have the knowledge or the skill to go into space. This world is all we will have. If we fail it, we will be among the species that are listed as extinct.

Tomorrow we will land on the planet.

Britt was right.

This world *is* our true Atonement.

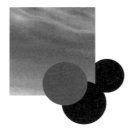

More Tales from the Wonder Zone...

Stardust

With a special introduction by the NEBULA AWARD-winning author of *Timescape*, *Cosm*, and *Eater*, Gregory Benford.
ISBN 1-55244-018-4

> The light of an alien sky...a hidden thief...a planet's living curse...
> the discovery that shakes the world...and a very different summer's
> night...

"Alien Games" *by Annette Griessman*
The colonists would have to leave. Diplomacy had failed and all hope was lost. Or was it? Who'd have thought playing a game could be the key to their future?

"Looking Through Glass" *by Mark Leslie*
The inventor was a genius, a genius whose best work was being stolen time after time. Then he discovered that to catch a secret thief, he needed a new way to see.

"The Doom of Planet D" *by Alison Baird*
It was a world of ancient cities and abundant wildlife. It was beautiful. It was appealing. It was much too good to be safe.

"Catching Rays" *by James Van Pelt*
Take a friend, a room filled with gadgets, and a curiosity the size of a mountain. Add a little something mysterious — and you could change the world.

"Shine" *by Beverley J. Meincke*
Ever looked at a computer screen and wondered what might be looking back? Be careful what you wish for!

Explorer

With a special introduction by the legendary C.J. Cherryh, Hugo and Nebula Award-winning author of the Foreigner and Fortress series.
ISBN 1-55244-022-2

> Alien visitors who can't leave...a dangerous vacation on the Moon...
> the not-so-lost civilization...discovering one's inner self...and a
> stranger who could change your life...

"The Snow Aliens" *by Derwin Mak*
First contact. A moment of incredible emotion and importance. There's just one problem. No one can find the aliens!

"MoonFuture Incorporated" *by Pat York*
It was supposed to be a vacation, until the accident. The Moon was supposed to have no surprises left. But there were.

"The Word Unspoken" *by Marcel Gagné*
The machines were silent, the homes abandoned, but the mystery remained: who were the long-vanished aliens? Where did they go? Someone should have asked: were they coming back?

"By Its Cover" *by Isaac Szpindel*
He wanted to be special. He wanted everyone to notice him. The doctor had the means. Could he pay the price?

"Rain, Ice, Snow" *by James Alan Gardner*
Just an old man. Or was he? With a harmless hobby. Or was it? An act of kindness. Or was it the only way to save the world?

Packing Fraction and Other Tales of Science and Imagination   ISBN 1-895579-89-9

A town is missing, but solving the mystery could be too dangerous...
She only wanted to be popular. Could she afford the price?...
A simple meteor impact turns out to be anything but ordinary. Working for aliens can make a tough job almost impossible...
And a busy executive wants a vacation where no one can reach him...

Available from your local bookstore or direct from the publisher.
To order, visit www.fitzhenry.ca • e-mail: godwit@fitzhenry.ca
telephone: 905-477-9700 • toll-free: 1-800-387-9776 • fax: 905-477-9179